ASYA AND CHRISTINE

A NOTE ON THE AUTHOR

Thomas McCarthy was born in Cappoquin Co Waterford and educated at University College, Cork. He has published four collections of poetry, *The First Convention* (1978); *The Sorrow Garden* (1981); *The Non-Aligned Storyteller* (1984); *Seven Winters in Paris* (1989) and one novel, *Without Power* (1991). He was the recipient of the 1991 O'Shaughnessy Poetry Prize of the Irish-American Cultural Institute.

ASYA AND CHRISTINE

Thomas McCarthy

POOLBEG

First published 1992 by
Poolbeg Press Ltd
Knocksedan House,
Swords, Co Dublin, Ireland

© Thomas McCarthy, 1992

Poolbeg Press receives assistance from
The Arts Council / An Chomhairle Ealafon, Ireland.

ISBN 1 85371 175 6

A catalogue record for this book is available from the British Library

Cover design by Pomphrey Associates
Set by Richard Parfrey in ITC Stone Serif 9.5/15
Printed by The Guernsey Press Company Ltd, Vale, Guernsey, Channel Islands

To Molly Keane

PROLOGUE

On a late afternoon in May 1924, Paudie Glenville arrived for the first time at the steamers' quay in Cappoquin. The riverside town quivered and floated in the bright sunshine. The Blackwater was at full tide, immense at its tidal elbow, expectant. The quay was filled with the aroma of cut rhododendrons and crushed laurel leaves that had been brought upriver for the May processions. Bags of potatoes and sacks of feeding-oats were banked together on the pitch-planks of the quayside. As soon as the schooner, the *Nellie Fleming*, docked, a huge basket spooned salt from the hold. Workmen from the local bacon factory walked with filled creels to waiting carts. There was a great urgency to the work because the boat had to get away quickly before the tide turned; otherwise it would be trapped in the low-tide sandbanks between Cappoquin and Youghal.

Glenville noticed a train passing along the recently repaired viaduct across the river. Because of the din from the quay, the train seemed to glide silently, as if in a film or a dream. It was laden with passengers: a company of soldiers of the national army withdrawing to barracks; scores of young men and women making their way to the bigger ports. The countryside, which had suffered so much during the recent war, was again being denuded by the relentless suction of trains.

Glenville thought about all the Irregulars he had sent away. By December of 1923 he had helped more than twenty volunteers to leave Ireland on the White Star liners *Celtic* and *Baltic* and the Cunard line's SS *Scythia*. He had thrown fifteen Mauser rifles, ten .22 revolvers and four hundred rounds into the sea between Youghal and Helvick.

Glenville had been a secret banker of two IRA columns, but he had never become a member of the IRB. He had never felt the need to be a member of a sworn circle, despite Michael Collins's offer to all IRA men that they could become members of the secret organisation without being vetted. His sympathies lay with Cathal Brugha and Terence MacSwiney, who tried to have the IRB dissolved when Dáil Éireann came into being. The Civil War, the defeat of de Valera and the rounding up of fifteen thousand Irregulars, had come as a consequence of the enmity between Collins and de Valera. But de Valera had spoken now. The fighting was over. Peace and reconstruction had begun by the early summer of 1924.

All Glenville's worldly goods were contained in two huge tin and wooden trunks that he left at the quayside. He strolled away towards the busy town. He felt lucky. Because he had never appeared on an IRB list he hadn't been touched during the Civil War. He had avoided the humiliation and trauma of Mountjoy Jail and Tintown, just as he had escaped Frongoch seven years earlier. His parents had been killed in the Free State shelling of Youghal, but he looked upon their death as an accident, death by fire, a drowning in history. He wasn't looking around for anyone to blame. He knew the name of the officer commanding the Free State battery; he could easily have had him killed. Even now, it occurred to him, he had access to men who would relish an assignment of revenge. Many of the young volunteers who had filtered through his lifeline to the ports were ablaze with hatred, their hearts blackened by fratricidal enmity. He was glad to have syphoned them to New York and Boston. America would calm them down.

Ahead of him on the road to Cappoquin there was a young woman walking. She was burdened by her baggage and moved slowly. He couldn't help noticing her lovely figure; so lovely that even the prudent starched material couldn't quench it. From the cut and colour of her dress, her deportment, something about her manner, he could see that she wasn't a local girl. He guessed that she must be a foreigner, an English or Scottish maid for one of the Big Houses that had survived the Troubles. But then he heard her shouting. "Damn! Damn, blast it!"

He quickened his pace to catch up with her and addressed her boldly. "I'll take one of those cases. I have only the one small case."

"Are you a peddler? Listen, I've no change to give you. Go away now, go on." She looked at him fiercely. She was no lamb.

"I'm not looking for anything from you."

"That's a relief. Thank you, so. Do take one." He took

the bag from her. She stared at him, studying him like a cattle-buyer.

How would he begin with her? What was the best thing to say? He felt like an ignorant countryman. But he summoned up the courage. After all, it was early summer. The afternoon stretched before him, warm enough to experiment.

"Are you coming home from America?" he asked, looking straight at her, trying to catch her eye.

"My father was supposed to meet me when the schooner reached Killehala." She looked straight ahead as she spoke; her examination of him had already concluded. "I'm sure he got drunk and forgot about me. It has taken me two days to get from Cork to here. The railway line is cut again near Cork. I thought the war was supposed to be over...I'd have been faster walking."

"You're travelling light," he said, not meaning to make it sound the way it did; double-edged.

"I suppose you think I haven't done well in America," she replied sharply.

"Not at all, none of my business." He was embarrassed.

"That is so true. But if you wish to know, I have four trunks of clothes waiting for me in Cork. And I have dresses and woollens and lovely Nebraska quilts that my aunt is keeping for me in New York." After a short pause she added," I can make a list if you need one."

He grinned with amusement. His tanned face, marred only by a blue mole above his upper lip, turned to her again. When he raised his head his sloe-coloured eyes filled with sunlight. She stared back at him, full of an American confidence.

"You do look lovely in that dress," he said, without conviction.

She sniffed, a sniff of disapproval and dismissal. She hardly ever sought compliments, and was not impressed by unsolicited ones. "Tell me," she asked, "if you're not a peddler, what are you?"

"I'm going to start a business. I have some capital."

"My father is convinced that this is a bad place—and a bad time—to start anything. The Troubles aren't fully over yet. My father says the British still haven't handed everything over to the native business interests. And thousands of workers have lost their jobs since the British garrisons left. All that business is gone north to Ulster. Farm prices are dropping too. My father's letters were full of the woes of farming."

"Well, I've made my bed. I bought two forges left behind by the British at Cappoquin. Some old coachhouses as well. They are near the railway line, on the embankment."

"When I was a child the people round here called it 'the bank.' So you are a blacksmith, a strong man. Which is why you go around offering to carry people's baggage."

"No, I'm a carpenter. My father was a coach-builder in Youghal. He died in the war."

"The Great War, is it? I always wanted to be a nurse in Belgium or France."

"Not that war. Our own Troubles. My father was killed in the Free State shelling of Youghal." He was disappointed that she didn't show any emotion. "It was only a year ago," he added, in an attempt to move her.

"I'm sorry. I am truly sorry for you. I don't know what I'd do if my father died. He is so incompetent and he is a drunk, yet I love the scoundrel. But I hope you're not one of those Irregulars, the ones who try to destroy our native government."

"I don't want to destroy anything," he replied bluntly. "I'm starting a business; I've planted my capital in this country." He looked at her luminous red dress again. What a startling colour, in this place and at this time of day. What a brazen young woman. America must have made her so forthright. He gave her a searching, serious look. "And your name, I didn't catch your name," he muttered.

"It wasn't offered, so you couldn't catch it," she replied. "But my name is Adele, Adele Griffith. I think the name is German, it means 'noble.'"

"Glenville is my name. Paudie Glenville. Don't ask me what 'Paudie' means. I couldn't tell you."

He thought that she had grown into her name, her head held high and her body erect and unconquered.

"Isn't it lovely to have a brand new country," she said suddenly. It was an exclamation, not a question. "To be alive on a May afternoon like this. When you think of all the Irishmen who never came back from the war, the Great War, I mean."

"They're not the important ones now," he said angrily. "Their deaths were wasted, wasted when they could have stayed at home and filled the ranks of the Republic."

"At least the Memorial Book was published just in time," Adele said. "They won't be forgotten entirely. I had eight first cousins and two uncles who died in France. My father lost both his brothers."

"My parents were murdered with British ammunition in Youghal."

"Look!" she exclaimed. She pointed to the new Swiss-style house that had been built for the parish priest. It overlooked the bend in the river. "Isn't it beautiful! My father gave me a complete account of its construction. He is a woeful drunkard, but he wrote such wonderful letters."

"You are a lucky woman." Paudie Glenville had never received a letter from his father. In the years since the beginning of the War of Independence he had led the life of a nomad, moving from house to house, shifting sums of money between Cork and Waterford and Tipperary. Unlike those of Miss Griffith, his arrivals and departures were neither recorded nor awaited by close relatives.

A horse and wagon carrying a consignment of butter rattled past, almost hitting Adele. "Careful!" he shouted. He had time to read the name on the sideboard: Watson and Son, Exporters, Lismore.

"There he is!" she shouted suddenly, unaware that she'd nearly been run over. She dropped her baggage and ran towards a horse and side-car that had turned off the main Lismore road.

"My dear child! My own daughter!" the driver cried as he drew near. He was a heavy man with a red face and the look of a prosperous tenant farmer. Adele raced into his arms. There was no mention of Killehala, missed connections, irresponsible fathers.

"Thank you, Mr Glenville," she said after she had disengaged herself from her father. "You were very kind."

"I did nothing."

"You did. You spoke to me kindly when I didn't feel kindly towards menfolk. You were very kind to me."

Her father seconded the vote of thanks, after judicious hesitation. "Thank you, young man. What are you doing in these parts? Are you a traveller?"

"No, I've bought the forges at Cappoquin. I'm going into business."

"Damn and blast it, it's a bad time for business here. There's a lot of labour trouble. Workers striking everywhere, they think we still have the money like we had in the Great War. The workers around here want to take our land and our cattle from us. Bloody Bolsheviks. The Farmers Freedom Force is trying to put manners on them."

"Don't be frightening the man before he even gets started, Dada," Adele laughed.

"Anytime is a bad time to start in business, if you're not prepared for a lot of knocks," Glenville replied philosophically. He thought that the life of conflict had been put behind him. He wanted to be left alone to make money.

"I'm quite serious," the father continued. He had been drinking. "Labourers have taken over creameries around here and in Tipperary. If the national government was any good they'd blast the lot of them out of it. We didn't win freedom for our country just to hand everything over to labourers."

"Dada, you didn't put yourself out during the fight for freedom. You sold to the IRA and the British garrison with equal fervour." Adele poked fun at his passion.

He roared with laughter, still happy that she hadn't given him a lecture on drink and pubs. It was usually the first topic when he met any of his relations. Mr Glenville had proved a very useful distraction.

"I'll be off," Glenville said. "I hope I can get a room in Fraher's Hotel."

"That's in Cook Street, on the way to the station."

"I know it," Paudie replied.

"Good luck to you," Adele said.

They parted abruptly, as if they didn't know the right way to disengage. He was impressed by the sincerity of her good wishes. "Maybe we could..." But it was too late. The Griffiths, a family once more, had thrown a cordon of indifference around themselves.

੨ଈ

When Glenville arrived at the forges he was pleasantly surprised. The property was bigger and in better condition than he had remembered. He had visited the place in 1920 after dropping money to an IRA group. It was good to walk around now with all the foreigners gone. There was an expanse of courtyard, and an eerie silence in the stables. The British military withdrawal had been orderly, but the Irish civilians who had manned the forges and stables left behind their implements, overcoats and rotting baskets.

At the base of one workbench he found a crushed gold ring; whoever had been working on it must have been startled and fled. He placed the ring on an anvil and prised it open with the aid of a bolt and a hinge. There was an inscription: Robert, 12/7/1918. Who was Robert? he wondered. Had the ring been stolen from a British soldier. When he had rounded it as best he could he tried to fit it on one of his fingers. It wouldn't fit. Then it occurred to him. Of course, Robert was the giver. It was a woman's ring. He put it in his pocket. A flock of pigeons, frightened by his hammering, climbed laboriously into the sky. He inspected the grates and the big metal and leather bellows. Nothing had been damaged. There was nothing to worry about apart from damp stains in the inner chimney walls. There was a danger that the furnace linings would crack when the fires were lit again. He would have to heat up the grates gradually. He then walked across the gravel courtyard to inspect the living quarters, the former sergeant-housekeeper's house. Most of the garrison had lived in a barracks that had been sold separately for conversion into an hotel.

While he was walking across the yard a tall man arrived, leading a white donkey.

"Well, hello!" the visitor shouted. "You must be the poor soul who's going to buy all this."

His donkey snorted. It had white socks and a white patch over its left eye. It was tackled with a simple snaffle-bit.

"I'm the very man," said Glenville.

"I'm John Hogan. I used to do smithy work for the old garrison. Will you be looking for a man?"

"I will surely, and that donkey of yours, is he part of the bargain? There's a lot of cleaning up to do."

The next day Hogan came back, his donkey harnessed

to an unsprung trap. The two men set to work straight away, working themselves and the poor animal to exhaustion, clearing the stables of rotted straw and mouldy grain, and the forges of baked horse-shit, lengths of iron pipe as well as torn trousers and old photographs. During a tea-break they fitted one photo together; it revealed a semi-naked woman eating what looked like a ceramic apple. "A soldier's plaything," said Hogan disapprovingly. "No wonder they were all beaten out of the country."

"We all have those weaknesses, John."

Because the work was endless and his boss seemed an agreeable man, Hogan arrived one morning with a companion. The new man's name was Paddy Kenny. He carried his small son, Ned, on his shoulders. The second man was hired and Hogan's donkey was bought outright.

On the fourth Thursday after Paudie's arrival, a fair day in Cappoquin, Miss Griffith paid them a surprise visit. The three men were working on a heavy iron gate for Sir John Keane's farm when they saw Adele standing at the entrance to the forge. Her clothes were more sober. The fastidious darkness of the countryside had begun to dampen her style.

"All my trunks arrived from Queenstown!" she roared above their hammering.

Glenville was surprised to see her. For some idiotic reason he thought they might not meet again. "My God, Adele. Did you come into town with your father?"

"What wonderful questions you ask! I came to town on an elephant." She winked at John Hogan. "Do you not go to Sunday Mass, Mr Glenville?"

"Not since Archbishop Walsh and the hierarchy

condemned Republicans."

"Do I detect a note of bitterness, a little tiny unChristian note of hatred?"

"Republicans were excommunicated." He left the workplace and approached her. His hands were dirty. He couldn't shake her hand.

"Republicans could always ask for forgiveness." She smiled at him as she spoke. She didn't give a damn about Republicans or Free-Staters or anything else from the Godforsaken past. But she had found something that rattled him; politics were an emotional lever that gripped his attention. She liked to engage him completely and instantly. It was like playing with a lively young colt.

"The bishops haven't asked for our forgiveness yet."

"The sin of pride is the worst sin."

"That's what we said to the bishops when they excommunicated us."

"Us? Us? What's all this 'us?' Have you formed a committee?"

"I'm not involved in anything," he replied, removing his leather apron.

They walked together towards the living quarters.

She was surprised to see that he had settled in so quickly, but her surprise turned to amusement when she saw how badly he looked after himself. The large stove in his kitchen hadn't been repaired so he boiled water and fried greasy suppers on the open fire of what passed for a sitting-room.

"Will you have a cup?" he asked, meaning tea.

She sat on a scruffy armchair and awaited his offering.

"Is your father buying or selling at the fair?"

"My father is probably just spending, drinking himself into an early grave," she explained wearily.

He offered her a cup of tea. The tea was horrible. The water hadn't been boiled properly. When she drank it she felt sick. He watched her while she played with the cup of grey liquid. She was quiet.

"I've had so many imaginary conversations with you these last few weeks," he said suddenly. "It's very quiet around here when the others go home. The town itself is quiet. They still have to get over the loss of the British. I've a lot of bad things to say about the Crown Forces, but this I will admit; they were good for business, they brought life into a place. They say that Fermoy is a ghost-town now."

"What kind of conversations?" she looked up at him kindly.

"Ah, you know, about how things are going. Sometimes I imagine myself talking to you about friends, dead friends." He looked at her sheepishly.

"Why didn't you visit me? We're not more than half an hour's walk away. You foolish man, if it's talk you want I'm always at home."

He sat down beside her and they talked. It was mainly his talk; the story of his life, his fight for Irish freedom, his memory of dead friends and past horrors, his guilt at never having done time in prison. She was bursting with things to tell him, but she held back. Let today be his day. Tomorrow or the next day, or next Sunday or next month he will get my memories of America. Then he mentioned her father again.

"Don't depress me by mentioning that man. He's a

scoundrel, a cruel and hard farmer. Farming is a hard life for a woman. I'd hate it."

He laughed, and touched her fingers with his. It was a split-second contact, unconsciously precise, as if her fingers were the ivories of a piano touched lightly. "I'm afraid I know nothing about farms," he explained. "I'm a townsman from Youghal."

"You're lucky then."

"Will your father be wondering where you are?"

"Let him wonder. I'm staying here until he comes to get me. Let him find me."

She tried to make herself comfortable in the battered armchair. "I feel at home here." She smiled at him. "Paudie, I do feel a migraine coming on. I'm not moving from this spot. I've had terrible trouble with headaches since I got scarlet fever in New York. That's why I came back home. My aunt got too frightened. She thought I was going to die on her. She was afraid that my father would blame her."

"Adele, will you be all right? Is there something I can do? Do you need water?"

"For God's sake, don't fuss." She raised her arm in a gesture of annoyance. "Would you leave me to rest? If I close my eyes for half an hour the headache will pass. It's not a bad one, I don't feel sick. You go back to your work."

He left her there to rest.

When he came back an hour later she was gone.

She returned regularly after that. They talked more and more, about her nursing in New York, her domineering aunt, the terrible poverty and ugliness of the immigrant quarters. He told her about his dead parents. He described for her the harsh poverty of the many country families who had sheltered him during the Troubles. He spoke about events that he had witnessed, terrible things, but he spoke about them as if they belonged to the distant past. The past had been put aside. Apart from his abiding love for Dev everything had been superseded.

"You talk about these things as if you were shell-shocked. It's possible, you know. You're not a cruel man at all; maybe you'd have been better off if you were."

"We're both outsiders here," he said as he laid a heavy calloused hand on her left shoulder. He sensed that her shoulders were taut with tension. "I've said too much to you, woman. You're getting too many of my worries."

Then she embraced him, tightly, and with a deep sigh. There was an element of desperation in her embrace. "I do worry about you. Won't they find you? The people who come in at home are so angry with the IRA, the Irregulars. Won't they catch you?"

"Who will catch me?" He looked down at her anguished face.

"The Free State army, the CID, those Special Branch men who are after the IRA now."

"Adele, nobody has anything on me, no letter, no address, no file at all. The only people who know my name and what I was doing are in America, in Albany and Chicago and places like that. My name is safe with them. Anyway, the country is settling down now. People who fought on the Free State side are rushing into business. Sure, I'm just like one of them the way I rushed into business."

He ran his left hand down her back. His hand rested at

the waist-band. Very tentatively, he caressed the base of her back.

❧

One day in late October, he and Adele and her father stood in a paddock full of dry cattle. It was a cold day. Their breath made patterns in the air. The three of them watched a servant-girl carrying two buckets of water across the farmyard to the kitchen. Glenville turned to the father. "Adele and I must marry. We only know each other five months, but we must marry. We want to."

"I'm going to have a baby, Dada." Adele touched her father's elbow gently. Then she gripped it.

Her father moved violently as if he'd been struck by a falling branch. Then he spoke without anger. "Dear, dear, child, what would your poor mother say? And what would your aunt say? They'd say I couldn't mind you for a few months in the country. After your aunt minding you so well for years in America. We'll wait and see. Couldn't you go back to America?"

"Dada, I'm marrying Paudie Glenville."

"But who is he? What are his people, what do you know about them? Nobody knows anything about him." He turned to Paudie for an answer. "You say you're from Youghal, but who are your people in Youghal? I never heard of any coach-builders in Youghal."

"My parents were murdered in Free State shelling. My family is scattered. Some of them are in America."

"Then who'll be your best man? Answer me that, answer me that one."

[16]

"To be honest with you, Mr Griffith, I never gave that a thought. I suppose John Hogan, the blacksmith, or the young tailor, Ned Lonergan. We're good friends."

"Has my daughter met any of your people?" he continued. He turned to his daughter. "Well, Adele? Have you met any of his people?"

"Wasn't I lucky enough to meet him? Wasn't God good enough to me that day?"

Her father looked away. The cattle had come towards them out of curiosity. The animals nudged against them, then headed for the railings that separated the field from the yard. "It's just, it's just that we don't know a thing about Paudie," he implored her. "I'm not used to dealing with people of no background. I know we've lived in troubled times. But people have to have some background."

"You take plenty of free drink from people of no background," Adele replied harshly. "He's going to be the father of your grandchild; isn't that all the background he needs?"

❧

They were married quietly in early December. The following May a healthy boy of eight pounds caused screams and havoc as he emerged from her petite frame.

"Could we call him Robert?" Paudie asked, thinking of the battered ring at the base of the workbench. Adele now wore it.

"It's a bit English, isn't it?"

"No, I think it's more Scottish than English," the father assured her.

"Right, that'll be his name. No more about it. Robert. Robert." Adele's voice was weak with exhaustion, but her mouth was fixed in a moist smile.

"You should plant a tree to celebrate your son's arrival," Dr White suggested.

A beech tree was planted. It grew quickly with the child, so that in the years that followed stray pigs, Walshe's white geese, Jimmy Foley's greyhounds and Brunnock's bullocks from Pound Lane all fed on the harvest of beech-nuts in Glenville's courtyard.

Glenville and Company moved on from the manufacture of gates to the fabrication of animal cages, coach-fitting and coach-building. Eighteen men and boys were employed, sons and daughters were born, so that in time the family became solidly bourgeois. Even the bibulous Mr Griffith became reconciled to his son-in-law, especially when he saw his daughter and her children being driven in a fine leather-upholstered Wolseley Saloon by one of the workmen from the Glenville yard, its eighteen horse-power engine roaring into the farmyard.

From the cocoon of this busy personal life Paudie Glenville watched the rise and fall of the third Sinn Féin party, the founding of de Valera's new organisation; and the growing prosperity of those who remained apolitical. He kept his head down, for the sake of his family, and to safeguard the few local government contracts that became available. He knew all about the Free State blacklists of ex-Republicans who sought jobs or contracts. He didn't wish to become involved.

But one July day in 1930 a man called Briscoe pulled up

outside his office in a dusty old Ford.

"For the life of me," the man complained, "Lemass will have all our backs broken. He must have bought these motors from tinkers." Mr Briscoe pushed a bundle of copies of *The Nation* into his arms.

"I've got those already," said Paudie.

"We're starting a daily newspaper. I'm collecting for the fund. We will never get the Republican point of view across otherwise. All the editors are afraid of Cosgrave."

"Maybe they're telling people what they want to read."

"Never! Never!" Mr Briscoe was adamant.

Glenville donated fifty pounds, a very generous sum. As a result of this he was sucked into the emerging community of Fianna Fáil. Adele eyed all of this with great suspicion and with increasing fear. She held him back. Twice, during the elections of 1932 and 1933, she persuaded him to refuse Party offers. Finally, he accepted a nomination on to the Party panel during the election campaign of 1938. Adele was devastated. In over thirteen years of marriage they had spent only four days apart.

"What about the business?" she demanded. "It isn't just your own life now, you know. You must think of the livelihoods of eighteen men. They have so many mouths to feed."

He looked at her, guilt in his face. He knew that he was doing this for himself. Something restless in him had been stirred. "I've gone over everything in my head. I've thought about the business over and over again."

"And?" Adele pressed him.

"I'm certain everything will be all right while I'm in the

Dáil. That's if I'm elected."

Adele couldn't look at him, she was so angry. She stroked a sprig of aromatic rosemary, while Runan, her five-year-old, played with her watch. They were sitting outdoors. "It's a terrible risk to take. Terrible. You said you were finished with all that in 1924. We are so happy. Doesn't it mean anything to you?"

"Good God, it means everything."

"Tell them you won't run, so."

"I have to run. I more or less said I would. Look, Paddy Kenny knows everything about the office. And Ned, his son, will be a great help to him. Young Ned has a great flair for figures. The business has its own momentum now; provided nobody's dishonest it won't fold because I'm away. I'll be back every Friday."

"That's big of you," she said bitterly. "What about your children?"

"They'll be fine. Just you see, Adele."

Adele stood up and brushed down her child-crumpled clothes. As far as she was concerned it was the collapse of the world she and Paudie Glenville had created together, an immensely private, comfortable world. For thirteen years or so she had felt completely fulfilled, and so happy that at the back of her Catholic Irish mind she had this nagging feeling that it couldn't last. Now politics had come to confirm her fears. Politics would rob her of this serious and steady husband. If he was elected he would be everyone's husband, and his family would be the last item on his constituency list. He would be coming back to Cappoquin each Friday all right, but he wouldn't be coming home.

"Do it if you must," she said as she turned to walk back into the house.

CHAPTER ONE

MARCH 1943

Five young officers of the Irish army were discussing the news of the latest Allied bombing that they had heard on the club wireless. The early-afternoon sun shone on the cold veranda of the boathouse. Taking their drinks outdoors was their way of showing the locals that they were hard men. That March there had been Allied victories in North Africa and Russian advances in the East. In Europe the great beasts of the night, the Lancasters and Halifaxes of Bomber Command, had penetrated deep into Germany. Berlin was burning. The wireless had just reported that fires could be seen from as far away as Bremen, a distance of two hundred miles.

"The Germans will find a way out of this," a young lieutenant from Wexford said solemnly. "They'll invent something. You'll see. They always do. The Germans are brilliant."

"They are on the run now. The Germans of old might have been brilliant, but these Nazis are completely daft," Lieutenant Kiely insisted. "You can't last if you're led by a dictator." Kiely's hair was ruffled by the wind, his pale blue eyes moistened by the cold.

"How can you call the man a dictator? Isn't he hugely popular with his people? Hasn't he built his country up from the ashes?" demanded an older officer who'd come into the army from a farm in Co Meath.

"If you had read anything...If you had read anything written over the last ten years you'd see that he's a tyrant. He's a little dictator, I tell you, a tyrant."

"Take it easy, Kiely," said the captain. "You're in uniform now." He stared across the table in disapproval. "Another thing, Herr Hitler is not little. I saw him myself nine years ago."

"Christ! Where did you see him?" asked the young Wexfordman.

"In Munich. I was coming home from a camping holiday in Austria. My uncle met me in Munich; we were travelling together to catch the Dutch ferry to England." The captain lifted his beer-glass from the white slats of the veranda table. "'Twas the week of my twenty-fourth birthday. As a birthday present my uncle took me to a place called the Ostaria Bavaria. A restaurant, you know. That's where I saw Herr Hitler. He was with four other fellows. He walked across the floor to a corner table."

"I always thought he was small."

"Ah, that's just Allied propaganda. They try to make him a figure of fun. In fact, he's five foot and nine inches. Then, I suppose, I'm no giant myself."

The others laughed.

"He was very pale," continued the captain, "and he wasn't wearing a uniform. He wore a grey suit and a white shirt. Very neat, I thought."

"What was he eating?" one of the others asked.

"I don't remember. I tell you I just remember one thing. His forehead, it was jutting out. Not beautiful, not noble like the Germans. My uncle said that he had the bone-structure of someone low-born. More like a Fianna Fáil man!" he laughed, looking at Lieutenant Kiely. The lieutenant, whose forehead was high and noble, laughed along with the others.

Just then, Bobby Glenville, the tall skinny son of the Deputy, lost his balance on the slipway below the veranda. He fell through the loose boards of the pontoon landing-stage and carried a boat, the *Lady Alex*, with him. Two of the club oarsmen followed him into the icy water. There were curses of anger and shouts of pain from other men, as they tried to keep a second boat from slipping backwards. The young officers on the veranda looked down with amusement. Hoots of laughter came from their table. Their mocking laughter angered the Deputy's son, who had a quick temper. He raised his dripping arm and threatened them with a clenched fist.

"We'd beat ye lot sick!" he shouted. "We'd beat ye blind!"

The young officer from Wexford shouted back. "We'll see about that!" Lieutenant Kiely was going to shout some insult as well, but he felt the restraining arm of the captain. "No need to rattle him. He looks a proper eejit as it is."

The soldiers ignored the oarsmen after that. The locals, also, were too wet and cold to pick a fight. There would be other opportunities to get the soldiers, but not in daylight.

The incident was watched from the bridge that overlooked the boathouse by Chrissie, Bobby's sister, and her friend, Alice. They had been watching the club training session from their bridge-top vantage point. Eight men in various stages of undress were always good for a laugh. The March wind had forced Chrissie to wrap her mother's woollen coat more tightly around herself. Her mother didn't know that she'd borrowed the new coat. Chrissie didn't care: she felt she could handle her mother. She looked down on the boathouse again, and considered that the officers incongruously sitting in the cold were an added bonus. In their uniforms, with their cigarettes and the scattered Saturday papers, their chatter and the blaring wireless, they seemed very romantic.

It was Alice who said that they looked like something out of a London film.

"What happened down there?" Alice asked in her quiet voice.

"Bobby. Bobby as usual making an ass of himself. He started screaming at the soldiers. I wouldn't mind so much but that lovely Lieutenant Kiely is down there. You know the one that Mari Broderick tried to get her claws into at the St Stephen's Night dance in Tallow." Chrissie spoke through the woollen fabric because her mouth was covered. She had lips that were easily cracked by the cold.

"I've heard of him," said Alice.

"But that brother of mine," said Chrissie," I'm so ashamed of him. He's so embarrassing, Alice."

"He's not. He is hot-blooded, that's all."

Chrissie sighed, a heavy adult sigh that was full of the

weight of the world. "Will he ever be settled? You tell me that, will he ever be happy?"

She looked down at the river-bank where two oarsmen had upturned the *Lady Alex* on her iron outrigging. "My father was really hurt when Bobby left the monastery. He just fooled everyone for over a year. He just wanted to get out of home. The monks loved him and tolerated him even more because Dada is a TD. But imagine to go off without saying a word and to end up drunk in the Cats Bar! Imagine that!"

"Ah, he's only seventeen. You talk about him as if he was thirty."

"He's bloody well eighteen, and he should act his age."

"You're just too hard on him. You're all too hard on him. Your mother kills him. Hasn't he got all the time in the world?" Alice's eyes, darker than Chrissie's brown eyes, settled on her friend's face affectionately. She looked upon Chrissie as a younger sister. Chrissie was seventeen, Alice was twenty.

"Anyway, you're prejudiced," Chrissie said in accusation. "You know he has a soft spot for you. I've seen him looking. I have!"

"Don't be daft! He has never shown interest. He is totally absorbed in his sports. All that football and the boats and motor-bikes."

Chrissie gave Alice a dig in the ribs. "Why don't you encourage him, then? If he's not going to be a Cistercian priest he may as well start becoming a man."

A look of panic came into Alice's face. "Chrissie, I must never do that. I'm in your family's care until my own father returns from England. He might not be back for years. Then we'll be able to go back to Cork; or to Bradford if things don't work out in Cork. I can't flirt with Bobby. It's not that I don't want to...he's so lively and beautiful ...and musical. He has so much. I have so little. But the little I have is not for him, I think. My family is so complicated, Chrissie."

"He's interested, Alice."

"Don't make things more confused than they are. You are a terrible rogue, Chrissie!"

"You're cold, girl. You're just another cold Protestant!" Chrissie attacked her. Even as she spoke the words she knew they were stupid. But she couldn't recall them. "I'm sorry, Alice, I'm really sorry. You're my best friend; the first decent friend I ever had. But you keep so much to yourself. I get jealous because you don't need anyone."

"I need so much, Chrissie. You're lucky, you've such a big family. All those friends. I have no one. My father is a Jew, you know that. My mother was a Methodist. I don't think my parents ever understood each other. Even I remember them not being very close—and that's something, if you think that my mother died when I was eight. You are so lucky, the way you throw yourself into love. No, I just wouldn't know how to take a risk like that."

ع

A few hours later, young Lieutenant Kiely knocked politely on Deputy Glenville's door in Cook Street. Adele asked the young man to come inside. She called to Bobby, who was tinkering with the lately tuned piano in the sitting-room. When Bobby came down the hallway and learned about the Army challenge for the next day he was delighted. What he didn't know was that three of the army crew were also members of the Atlunkard and Shandon boat-clubs.

"We'll give ye the *Lady Alex*," he said. "It's our fastest frame, even in choppy water. But don't expect to win."

The young lieutenant thanked him profusely and got up to go. By then Chrissie had placed herself between him and the front door. Before he was allowed to leave he had to pass her inspection. When she looked at him close-up a part of her caved in. She gathered up enough breath to say hello.

"Barry, Miss," he said, and for a split second she almost knelt, she was so bewildered. "My name, it's Barry Kiely," he repeated.

You're beautiful, Chrissie said to herself, but not a word passed her lips until he had left.

"Are you stupid or something?" Bobby asked. "The man was trying to talk to you but you snubbed him. What kind of behaviour is that?"

Adele came out into the hall. "Is he gone already? And I thought he'd hold on until I talked to him about the Red Cross fund-raising." Then she turned to her son. "Bobby, if you've nothing better to do would you light the fire in the sitting-room before your father's train gets in."

Adele went back into the laundry, where Ellie, the maid, was ironing some sheets.

"Is he really a doctor, Mrs Glenville?" Ellie looked up from her work.

"Yes, he's a medical man, all right. Maybe he's only an aide. I don't know how the army works, Ellie."

"He's a beautiful dancer anyway."

"Is that so?"

"Yeah, I'm telling you no lie. Chrissie and me watched him dancing in Tallow on St Stephen's Night. The Brideside Serenaders were playing. He was like Fred Astaire the way he moved."

"Oh, Lieutenant Kiely, I'm in love with thee," Bobby sang from the hallway, teasing Chrissie.

"Go away from me, you tramp!" Chrissie shouted.

Bobby returned to the piano and played with the keys once more. He became more serious. He had spent the last few days listening to the music and words of Wallace's *Maritana* on the wind-up gramophone. He sang along with the record:

> In happy moments day by day
> The sands of life may pass...

When the record slowed down he cranked the gramophone with the silver crank-lever. A crackling Edwardian voice entered the room once more, filling the late afternoon with its mellow tones and making him ashamed of his own half-trained voice. The music had a calming effect on him; it opened up spaces of uncharacteristic peace, spaces within which he felt drawn to higher things, music or the religious life. While he was cranking the gramophone yet again little Emer burst into the room.

"What is it?" Bobby demanded.

"Declan is trying to start your bike!"

"The little eejit, doesn't he know there's no petrol?"

He abandoned the music. His fear was that Declan was messing with the Manx-Norton that his father had bought him for his sixteenth birthday. When he reached the bike-shed he saw Declan jumping off the pedal of a BSA scrambler. The bike shuddered with the force of the leap.

"Get away from that! Can't you see there's no petrol?"

He slapped Declan across the face, but Declan just backed away, laughing. The beautiful black-and-white 1937 Manx-Norton hadn't been touched. Declan had removed its hessian covers, but just to look. Bobby was relieved. The BSA was just a rough scrambler.

"Look, after the Emergency, or whenever we get petrol, I'll show you how to use the scrambler. But only if you promise to leave the Manx alone."

"Great!" Declan shouted and ran away.

Suddenly, they heard their mother calling from the kitchen. "Dada's home!"

Deputy Glenville had returned on the afternoon train, laden with Dáil papers and back numbers of *The Irish Times*. But the prize item was a pair of fresh oranges. He placed them on the kitchen table with all the pride of a vain chef.

"Two boxes went on sale at the Dublin fruit market. You should have seen the rush!"

"Look, Gerald," Emer said, trying to mother her little brother.

"Oranges," whispered Gerald, before going to the cutlery tray for a sharp knife.

"Go ahead and take one up. Feel the lovely skin, "Adele

coaxed him. But Gerald was too practical. His mind was already on the problem of division.

It was really the adults who were struck with a sense of awe by the presence of the oranges. Oranges represented a brave run through dangerous seas by one of the country's little ships. Last thing at night all the children were made to pray for the brave neutral ships that plied between Ireland and neutral Portugal.

"A section for everyone," the Deputy said.

He was glad to be home. Each train journey from Dublin was more exhausting than the previous one. Engines broke down, fuel had to be collected at intervals. By this time most of the deputies had become a little edgy. An election seemed likely. In the new year the leader of the opposition party had made a savage attack on government policy. He had accused the ministers of insufficient planning and supply, careless administration and botched rationing. Most significant of all, the opposition had promised to de-rate certain agricultural lands if they were elected. That was a real promise, a practical change, the first real sign that an election was in the air.

Since the Christmas of 1942 they had all waited for an announcement. The sense of expectation had intensified with the progress of the Dáil, the hurried reading and enactment of bills.

"We had a Lieutenant Kiely here today," Adele said. "Not long before you came in. The officers in the garrison want to row against the club."

"That's no contest, the club will trounce them," the Deputy replied.

"They seemed very confident. The young Kiely guy seemed full of himself." Bobby chewed on the section of orange as he spoke. The back of his hand shone with the glaze of the dripping fruit juice. "Our problem is that our two best men, Murray and MacLoughlin, are away with the army in Kilworth."

"He was very gentle, wasn't he?" said Emer.

"Who?"

"Lieutenant Kiely, who else?"

"He's a beautiful dancer," Ellie piped up. She took her place at the edge of the table, near the stove, where she could help to serve the Deputy's tea. She would wait until he asked for it. The kettle was boiling on the fast plate of the Aga.

"Bobby, I called into the workshops on my way up," the Deputy said to his son. "Ned tells me that you'll make a tidy welder. He said he put you in charge of two boys last week. That's good, good...good."

"Ned is always firing responsibilities at me. He really gets to me sometimes."

"He has to do that. It's his place to do it. In another year or two you'll have to take control of the business. Or an ancillary business. You can't walk away from these things." The Deputy looked at Bobby closely, scrutinising his face for a reaction.

Just then seven-year-old Gerald got up from his chair. "I'm going to vomit the orange. I'm tellin' ye!"

"Go and stand at the kitchen door," Adele shouted.

"Oh, dear!" said Ellie.

"Leave him, Ellie," Adele said. "He'll be grand."

While young Gerald was standing at the kitchen door, Alice arrived. Chrissie let her in through the front door and the two women arrived together at the kitchen where the household was feasting on an orange.

"How's my mangey old father?" Chrissie greeted the Deputy. "Did you bring me anything from Dublin?"

"Here's a piece of an orange."

"An orange! What good is an orange to someone my age? I'm not a child." She kissed him just the same, glad that he was home. "There were lovely skirts advertised in the *Press* last week. I meant to write to you. I suppose you didn't notice them. You're as blind as a bat when it comes to clothes." She pulled her father's ear playfully.

Alice, painfully polite, had remained at the door of the kitchen. Adele noticed this and beckoned to her. "Come in, child. Would you like a sandwich or something? Some tea?"

"Alice used to drink all kinds of funny teas in Cork before the Emergency," Chrissie said.

Bobby rose from his chair beside his father and told Alice to sit down. He poured a cup of tea for her.

Alice was extremely shy, and like most shy people drew attention to herself only by her little strategems. Although she looked a little like Chrissie, her formality and good breeding set her apart from the rough-and-tumble natives of the town. Her father was a prosperous Jewish businessman who had never recovered from the death of his unhappy wife. He had been an important and regular customer of the Glenville ironworks, becoming a close friend of the Deputy around the time of the Blueshirt movement.

Glenville had calmed Mr Schless after a particularly vicious attack on Jews and international bankers by General O'Duffy that he had witnessed while on a visit to Cork. He persuaded him not to worry; there was no tradition of strutting racists in Ireland and the Blueshirt thing was only farmers and Cumann na nGael people coping with the fact that they'd lost power in 1932.

Mr Schless often used the name Sloan; in fact, the Glenville business had often been paid by cheques signed by a Mr Sloan. Mr Schless had more accurate and more direct sources of information than Paudie Glenville. When the war broke out and England declared war on Germany he moved to the Leeds-Bradford area to take up what he euphemistically called "religious work." His daughter, whose birth-name was Asya Schless, was transformed into Alice Sloan, a Methodist from Cork, complete with birth-cert, school reports, ration books. Her father had bought a small house in Church Street in Cappoquin, where she moved in 1940. She lived alone, but under the Deputy's protection. If Ireland was invaded by the Germans there was a plethora of contingency plans to protect her or spirit her away.

She had often stayed with the Glenvilles, yet a part of her remained aloof. She couldn't be integrated into a boisterous family; she carried too much solitude within her.

"No milk, Bobby." She placed her hand over the cup. He needed constant reminding.

"Ned Kenny is coming over later," the Deputy said to Adele. He left the table, placing a hand on her shoulder as he passed.

"Politics, politics," muttered Chrissie.

"These aren't easy times," her mother began to defend the Deputy. "He knows how bad things are. There are going to be terrible shortages this year. Some people will go hungry before the new harvest. He knows that. And he's worried about the shortage of gas for welding. You must give your father a chance. He has terrible burdens now."

"He chose his burden," Chrissie replied sourly. "But you should tell him not to stand when the election is announced. The life is being drained from him."

"The Party doesn't want anyone to step down."

"You could get him to stand down."

"And have him hating us for the rest of his life. That, my love, is one thing we can't have."

That night two men from the local Party, Tom Lincoln and Ned Lonergan, called to the house. They wanted to know if rumours of the election were true. The Deputy didn't pretend to know more than they did. He said that Dev was keeping everything to himself. Even ministers were left in the dark. The only certainty was that there would be further cuts in the supply of petrol and other fuels.

While they were talking, Ned Kenny arrived. He was disappointed to find the others, having come in the hope of having a private audience with his pope. The others had to persuade him to stay. Ned was in his early twenties, but he had the gait and mental attitudes of someone much older. This was one of the reasons he was trusted by others. He was annoyed that there was no inkling of an election date. "Is there no indication at all? Surely you've heard something?"

"Not a blessed thing," the Deputy admitted.

"Damn it, you should spend more time with the other deputies. What do you be doing all day up in Dublin?"

"I do be looking after all the problems that you bring to me every time I come home." The Deputy threw a scornful look.

"You'll learn nothing coming home every bloody weekend. That's for sure." Ned had grabbed the Deputy's ankle and he wasn't going to let go.

"Surely the man has your permission to come home, to see his wife and family?" asked Ned Lonergan.

"And to see his own town of Cappoquin," Tom Lincoln added.

"I'm telling you now, a man has to be careful. Dev needn't be too sure of a big vote. I've been listening to the men in the yard. They're not too happy with the way things are. They could turn against Dev in a flash."

"Oh, I agree, I agree, Ned," Glenville said. "But there's a mountain of work to be done in Dublin. Meetin' with other deputies is sometimes a luxury I can't afford. There are just too many letters."

"Every letter's a vote," Tom Lincoln remarked ruefully.

"By the way, I met Captain Mulvey." Ned Kenny suddenly changed the subject. Mulvey was a retired merchant marine officer who operated a small steamer on the river. "He wanted to know if you'd attend the boat race between the club and the army tomorrow."

"I don't know," the Deputy muttered.

"Bobby was the one who more or less challenged the

army," Ned explained.

"Ah, I will, I will, I will." The Deputy, who had already committed himself to a Sunday-morning meeting in Lismore and a Sunday-afternoon scrutiny of the Glenville trading accounts, now committed himself to the boat race.

"Hello, serious men." Chrissie opened the sitting-room door and greeted the three men. "If ye're going to stay in here until tomorrow morning we may as well take the gramophone away. And the records." She marched across the room with Emer and Gerald. They rescued the gramophone from the spot where it stood neglected and retreated silently.

"She's very bold," the Deputy said. He was about to elaborate when she came back into the room.

"The crank. We forgot it," she said, taking the silver handle from the top of the piano.

"The young must have their music," said Ned Lonergan, without a trace of conviction.

"It's a pity they've no interest in our own native music," complained Tom Lincoln. "We live in a gramophone-deafened world."

"She'll be back for the needles," the Deputy said, smiling with satisfaction, shaking the frayed black cardboard box.

CHAPTER TWO

A large crowd gathered for the boat-race. On the river-bank
and club veranda, people huddled together against the
cutting March breeze. Deputy Glenville, Captain Mulvey,
two officials from the club and the commandant of the
local garrison stood in Captain Mulvey's boat. A starting-
line stretched ostentatiously from the craft to a white-and-
yellow marker buoy. The tide had just begun to turn and,
as it was ebbing towards Youghal against the breeze, the
water was choppy. Water licked and played with the oars
extending from dark blue gunwales. Captain Mulvey stood
erect and silent, his pistol pointing towards the heavens.
His black-and-white water-spaniel, Moll, stood ready to jump
and retrieve. But when the captain pulled the trigger there
was no response: the cartridge was wet.

"It's the only one on the boat," the captain said angrily.
"And that's the last cartridge in the club. Dear God."

"Here, blow this up and give it a punch." The Deputy
handed him a large brown paper bag.

"Are ye right!" the captain shouted to the two crews.
Before waiting for a reply he burst the brown bag. It made

an enormous bang.

"Good thinking," said the commandant to the Deputy.

The Deputy looked through his binoculars at the strained faces of the oarsmen. The crews had different styles. The local crew, with Bobby as stroke, had a faster rhythm but dipped their oars lightly in the water. The army crew stroked more sluggishly, but hit the choppy water like grave-diggers, shovelling up bucketfuls of the tide and straining the canvas of the *Lady Alex* with their ferocious method. The Deputy looked at his son, and was delighted to see the grim determination on his face. "Good," he muttered," good, good."

"Bobby is keeping a good rhythm," said Mick Sargent, one of the club officials.

"He is."

"My lads are putting more effort into it," the commandant said.

"It's very deceptive," Captain Mulvey explained. He bent down to haul his spaniel out of the water. She had bolted in when the bag exploded. "Up, Moll!" he said.

They could hear the cheers of the crowd in the distance, the loud roars of the soldiers and the shrill screams of the local girls. It was difficult to make out who was winning. The Deputy gave Mick Sargent his binoculars. "The officers will make it by a canvas," commented Mick.

"Show, give me them binoculars." The Deputy took the glasses and looked towards the blue-and-white buoys. "That young lieutenant has a fine stroke. He's no novice."

The commandant looked at the Deputy. "I think he rowed with Shandon. Certainly his father was an oarsman."

"The club is going to win it!" shouted the Deputy. "Good man, Bobby!"

"Not even a canvas in it though," commented Captain Mulvey. "Those soldiers rowed well. They gave us a fright."

They could hear the crowd cheering wildly. A number of uniformed men made their way down the slipway to draw the *Lady Alex* from the water. They took the fragile blades of the oars and pulled their officers against the landing pontoon. The club crew waited mid-river, their bodies arched over the oars, exhausted. They'd won, but they had got more than they bargained for.

☙

"Let's go and see the soldiers," Chrissie suggested.

She had been sitting with Alice and Ellie on the stone steps that led from the road to the river-bank. They had all cheered for Bobby, but Chrissie's seventeen-year-old heart was with the quiet lieutenant. His presence, his quietness and what she imagined as his loneliness had been with her all day. She had dragged Ellie out in the cold March day so that she wouldn't be alone with her secret. She needed to share her longings. She wasn't sure if Alice would be the person to tell. But Ellie had used the other two as camouflage for her own romantic activities. She knew that her woodcutter boyfriend, Michael Kavanagh, would pass by on his way to check the family pony that grazed the inch by the river.

"Do you expect Michael to pass by soon?" asked Alice.

Ellie was startled by Alice's directness. "I do. Don't tell

anyone. If my father found out he'd beat me."

"Of course I won't, Ellie."

"Are ye going to do it?" asked Chrissie mysteriously.

"I'll try to persuade him. Men can't think for themselves. Your mother is always saying that, Chrissie."

They moved down the steps towards the crowd. When they reached the door of the club they hesitated in fear of a male preserve. Two officers passed through carrying kit bags. Chrissie smiled at them, but instead of returning her smile they looked at the three women with a kind of severe curiosity.

"Let's leave it," Alice said nervously.

"I'm not afraid of them. They can go to blazes. My father was in this club before some of those soldiers were born," said Chrissie angrily. "I'm going inside." Just then the lieutenant came out, preceded by a private who seemed to be carrying his bag.

Chrissie moved to cut off the lieutenant's exit. The second time that weekend. "Everyone says that you have a beautiful stroke," she said quickly. "I'm Chrissie. Remember? Deputy Glenville's daughter. It was my brother's crew that beat you."

"It was a good race, wasn't it? A fair match." The lieutenant hardly noticed that his exit was cut off by three girls.

"Ah, you have a great stroke." Ellie added her voice to the cause. She stared at the buttons on his uniform. He was nearly a foot taller than the women. He looked at Chrissie again, a quick look, but long enough to see that she was pretty. She was noticed, acknowledged. Chrissie looked back firmly into his raw blue eyes.

"Thank you," he said. "I used to row when I was at university. Before he died, my father was a coach."

"I'm sorry," Alice said.

"What?"

"She's sorry your father's dead," explained Chrissie.

"Ah. I did a lot of it before I joined the army. Rowing, I mean. We've no boats in the army!" he added jocosely.

"And we never had a navy. Isn't that sad?" As Ellie spoke, she pinched Chrissie's arm, urging her to go on. An officer came out and winked at the lieutenant as he passed; but not before his eyes did a body search of all three women.

They waited for Kiely to speak again. He had a soft voice, not harsh and metallic like many of the other officers. They wanted him to speak.

"Well, I can't be hanging around here. It's really my day off," Ellie said suddenly. "I promised Michael."

"You're lucky, Ellie."

The lieutenant smiled at Alice. "I wasn't introduced to you," he said, ignoring the other two.

"Alice Sloan."

"Alice is from Cork," Chrissie explained. "She doesn't have a family around here."

"A fellow Corkonian!" The lieutenant was delighted.

"Come on," said Chrissie. "You're not going to start all that Cork tribal thing. It makes everyone in Waterford sick."

Chrissie was annoyed that his focus had switched to Alice. On St Stephen's Night he had danced with one of the Barron sisters, now he was more interested in Alice.

There was no justice in this world.

"That block before you come to South Terrace proper," Alice was explaining. "We haven't lived there for years. We left it soon after my mother died."

"Do you know Fred Astaire?" asked Chrissie, trying to keep the sense of desperation out of her voice.

"What?"

"Not personally...I mean his dancing." Chrissie swallowed hard.

"He's a bit of a drip, don't you think?" The lieutenant dismissed her.

"Was your father a good dancer, then?" Alice spoke in support of Chrissie's approach. She knew that Chrissie was dying to compare him to Fred Astaire.

"No, but my sisters had a wonderful talent for it."

"Sisters? How many have you got?" Chrissie asked.

"Four. All older than me. I'm the baby of the clan."

"Ah, that's why you're such a good dancer. We saw you in Tallow after Christmas..."

"You remember that night? I don't remember meeting you there. Who were you with?"

"Just a crowd of us from Cappoquin." She did her best to hypnotise him with her brown eyes. It seemed to work: he kept his eyes on her. "We heard that you were a doctor."

"Almost," he explained. "I have to finish my intern year. I wanted to be in the army when the Emergency was declared. Don't ask me why, none of my family was in the army before. Not even the British army. Maybe I just wanted to escape from my four sisters."

"Are they still at home?" Chrissie asked. She wondered

if he came from a non-marrying family. She guessed that he must be twenty-three, or maybe younger. In fact, he was twenty-five.

"Three are married now. My eldest sister didn't marry."

While Chrissie was thinking of something else to ask, the soldier who had carried his kit bag to the jeep appeared at the gate and shouted to him. The lieutenant looked up angrily. The soldier got the message and came down the steps before shouting out the army's business to all and sundry. "Sir, the new lot from Kilworth are due at three."

"Must go," the lieutenant said.

"You must, I suppose." Chrissie smiled at him. "You should get in touch with my brother or Mr Sargent about using one of the boats."

"That's a great idea. You don't think they'd mind?"

"Sure, why would they?"

"I'll be in touch, so. Chrissie, isn't it?"

"When?"

"Very soon," he said," or it might be too late."

Chrissie didn't know what he meant by that. It worried Alice too. Did it mean that the country might be invaded? Terrible things might happen.

"What do you mean 'too late'?"Alice challenged him.

"Oh, you know, battalions get moved around."

That was all he meant. Alice could have slapped his face. He had put the fear of God into her. If Ireland was invaded she would be cut off from her father.

The lieutenant moved away. They watched his swift progress up the steps, kept their eyes on him until he closed the blue gate of the club property.

"Well," said Alice, "we all know that Fred Astaire is a drip."

"Don't be mean. He's lovely." Chrissie said. "And he's so talented. He can do all those medical things and row as well."

"Isn't your Bobby as talented, for goodness sake? Can't Bobby do all those things and more?" demanded Alice.

Just then Bobby came up behind them. "Did my ears deceive me, or was it me I heard praised?" He linked arms with Alice.

"You're thick with vanity," said Chrissie.

"Cruel, cruel sister." The three walked out together towards the narrow blue gate.

They heard Ellie's voice calling. She and her boyfriend ran forward, excited. Ellie was out of breath, wheezing. She looked wretched in her threadbare coat. "Guess what, we're engaged. We're going to get married in September!"

"What about your father?" cautioned Chrissie.

"I don't care about him. We're getting married."

"Congratulations, Mick!" Bobby shook the young woodcutter's hand. "Mind you, I wouldn't take responsibility for this wild woman."

"Has your father any idea at all?" Chrissie repeated her question.

"No," said Ellie calmly. "Sir John Keane is going to give us a cottage on the Melleray road. It's near the woods. That's handy for Michael." Ellie coughed then, a slow racking cough. She bent over in an effort to get some air. Her fiancé looked on in horror, growing more horrified as the coughing went on. Suddenly Ellie snapped out of it.

"It's nothing, nothing."

"You must go to Dr White ·with that cough," Chrissie said.

"I will if it stays. Leave me alone, will you?"

"Yeah, leave her alone, Chrissie," Bobby said.

"You're a friend, Bobby."

"Look at this," said Michael, raising Ellie's hand.

"A ring!" Chrissie exclaimed.

"It was my mother's," Michael explained. "And before that it was my grandmother's." The ring was dark; dark gold burnished by generations of turf-smoke in riverside cottages. It had three stones set in it.

"They're not diamonds," the woodcutter apologised. "I don't know what they are, but they're not diamonds."

CHAPTER THREE

"What does it feel like, to be in love. Tell me the truth."
Chrissie turned to Ellie one afternoon when the house was
quiet. The two women had been trying on Adele's new
clothes in her bedroom. Ellie was lost in a loose-fitting
camacurl coat in airforce blue. It had cost eleven pounds
and fifteen shillings, a small fortune.

"It's like this." Ellie escaped from the coat and handed
it to Chrissie. She breathed heavily, coughed, then threw
her eyes heavenward like a statue of the Madonna. She
nearly fell over the earthenware bed-warmer. She took
Chrissie's hands and said, "Like this, like Scarlett O'Hara
and Rhett, you'd die for it. You'd never be able to fight it."

"I don't think I'll ever have a chance to love like that."

"Ah, don't give up. You're only seventeen. You're still
fairly young."

"I don't know. I think my chances have come and
gone."

"You mean that lieutenant. You have it bad for that
fellow. Sure, you haven't even started with him."

Chrissie looked out the window. She couldn't fight back

the tears. She sank to the pillow. Despair overpowered her.

Ellie ran to comfort her.

"I'll never get a chance with him. Why should he bother with me, I'm only a child."

"Stop crying, anyway. You could get Bobby to bring him to the house. Isn't Mrs Glenville in the Red Cross? Couldn't she fix it so that he'd have to come to the house?"

"My mother, is it?" Chrissie rose from the bed angrily, shaking off Ellie's comforting hands. "Are you trying to mock me, girl? If my mother found out how I felt she'd box me across the ears."

Ellie disregarded her rejection. "Look, there's plenty of time. He's not going anywhere and the summer is coming. You'll get your chance."

"He could have a girlfriend already, or be engaged for all we know."

"He hasn't anyone. I checked with the soldier who's always carrying his bags for him. There isn't anyone else."

There was the sound of a door opening downstairs.

"Your mother! We'll be crucified!" whispered Ellie. She panicked and ran to the wardrobe with some of the clothes. The room was a mess: coats on the floor, dresses crumpled, hangers empty.

"I'll head her off," said Chrissie. She ran to the bedroom door. "Mama!"

But it was Bobby who answered. He ran up the stairs and asked Chrissie if she wanted to come badger-baiting. He came into the room.

"Oh!" he exclaimed. "Mama will have a fit if she sees this."

"You keep your mouth shut, so," said Chrissie casually.

"We're going badger-baiting out in Salterbridge. Do you want to come? Hallahan's have lost two good dogs. Ned Kenny has located the set. Do you want to come?"

"We do not."

"Afraid of the blood, is it?"

⋙

Half an hour later, Bobby, Ned and two other men approached a high culvert near Salterbridge Wood. They had four terriers with them. The dogs snapped at each other, excited. There were several holes in the culvert and above these were ridges of red earth where the badgers had been excavating. Bobby picked up a terrier and shoved it into one of the holes. Ned picked up another and carried it by the head and tail to another opening. One of the men, Pat Hyland, a railway worker, placed his head to the ground, listening. Ned and the other man took their spades and waited for the signal.

"Are they ready?"

"Leave them a few minutes," Pat whispered.

After a while the two men started digging. They heard one of the dogs barking and soon the barks turned to shrieks of pain.

"It's Jip! The bastard has attacked Jip!" Ned shouted.

They dug more furiously, shouting to the dogs. "Get him! Help Jip! Lass! Help Jip!" They heard another terrier barking wildly. After a few minutes of digging and trenching, Ned shouted to Bobby to get the retrieving-tool. Bobby climbed the bank carrying a long-handled implement that had been made at the Glenville forge. The huge tongs was pushed into the trench. One of the dogs was hauled out, snarling viciously, blood pouring from its torn snout and chest.

"Poor old Jip," Bobby said. Then he shoved the tongs in again and clamped it upon a much bigger load. The tongs twisted but Bobby put more effort into the job, taking the weight of the badger. He hauled the huge grey mass from its hiding-place. The badger, a female, snarled in terror. Lass emerged from the set carrying a badger pup in her mouth.

The men were surprised by this.

"I thought they ate their young when they were threatened," Ned said.

"Not always," replied Bobby.

They shoved the captured animal into a sack and dragged it across a field to a waiting truck. They all hopped aboard and headed for the ironworks. Ned nursed Jip with a cloth steeped in gentian violet. The terrier whimpered.

"He'll be all right. A night's sleep by a warm fire and he'll be right as rain," Bobby said.

When they arrived at the yard all the men stopped working and came to look at the badger. It was chained by its hindquarters. It shivered and bristled with fear and anger. Word spread that they had caught a badger. Some of the workmen had already brought their own dogs. They pushed and dragged the badger to a corral made with unpainted gates. The animal was chained to a heavy tank in the middle. Then the dogs were let loose upon it. The badger kept its head low and fought bravely, though unable to move freely because of the chain. The dogs snarled and bit and screamed when the trapped animal hurt them with its teeth and claws. One dog was badly injured and someone picked it up. Two dogs were bleeding. The men chatted and cheered occasionally when a terrier emerged from the fray with a piece of badger-skin. Some of the men had flasks of tea and shared their beverage with Bobby.

One man handed a tumbler to Bobby. It contained a mixture of tea and whiskey. It was Mike Fennell. "The Russians are doing great in the East." He was a scholar of the war.

"The Germans need a few terriers like Jip!" Bobby laughed.

"Now you said it, boy."

When all the dogs were bleeding Ned Kenny stepped into the centre, carrying a heavy spade. He smashed the badger's head, edgeways, with the spade and the noise was suddenly diminished.

"He put up a good fight," Ned admitted.

"I don't think it was up to much," someone complained.

"It was a female, an auld mother weakened by the birth," Pat Hyland explained. "The young we pulled out of the set were nearly newborn."

"That explains it."

"Phone!" someone shouted from the office window.

Bobby turned and ran to the window of the office. "Who is it?" he demanded.

"It's your father, from Dublin."

Bobby ran inside and took the phone. "What's up?" he

asked without even greeting his father. He knew his father hated delaying on the phone.

"It's Jack Kennedy, the lad who works at the creamery. His mother was just on to me. He's been arrested."

"Jasus, what happened?"

"The authorities found a 42-pound box of butter in Kennedy's garden. He's made his position even worse by denying any knowledge of the thing. But he was being watched. The guards are holding him in the cell below in the barracks."

"I'll go down there now. Has his mother been to see him?"

"Not at all. The woman is afraid she'll be arrested if she goes down to see him. She asked me to do something. If you like you could take Ned Kenny with you."

"No, I'll go on my own."

Bobby left the others to clean up the badger mess. When he arrived at the barracks the guards were in sour humour.

"What sort of a generation of thieves are we after breeding?" the sergeant complained.

"His mother spoils him, that's all."

"We're going to keep him away from his mother. For a few hours at least. There's been a lot of trouble around here lately. A whole string of larcenies of butter, salmon, sugar, even grain. Can you believe that, grain being stolen? Anyway, he's going to stew in there for a while until he talks a bit more."

"My father phoned from Dublin," explained Bobby. "He was worried about Jack doing damage to himself."

"What kind of damage?"

"My father mentioned suicide. Kennedy's mother said that he tried to kill himself last summer. My father was worried about that. If anything happened the minister would blow a bloody fuse. With all the trouble over Republican prisoners starving themselves in jail."

That did the trick. Kennedy, a saucy, unbowed look on his face, was released pending a court appearance. Bobby was triumphant.

Bobby and Kennedy walked along Chapel Street towards Kennedy's house in Twig Bog Lane. The railings made them both think of prison. Kennedy would go to jail for the theft. Worse than that, he would never get another job. What an eejit, thought Bobby.

They had to step off the footpath because a child was playing a ball game against the high perimeter wall of the church grounds. It was Helen Nolan, a shopkeeper's daughter. The child hopped the ball rhythmically against the ground, then threw a second ball, all the time reciting:

> Archi balls balls balls
> King of the Jews Jews Jews
> Bought his wife wife wife
> A pair of shoes shoes shoes
> And when the shoes shoes shoes
> Began to wear wear wear
> Archie balls balls balls
> Began to swear swear swear.

CHAPTER FOUR

Bobby withdrew his hand from Alice's shoulder. Alice looked away in disappointment. This wasn't meant to happen. He is too young, she thought. How could she have allowed him to get so close? She was the mature one; she always felt that she could control the situation.

"I just think you're a great woman. That's all." Bobby scrutinised her face for a look of approval or disapproval. "I don't mean to make your life difficult. Will you forget this happened?"

"It's the atmosphere of this room, it's so warm and peaceful. And the gramophone. It's perfect." Alice excused him completely.

It was St Patrick's Day. The Glenville family usually went to the Griffith house, "Grandad's", on that day. But Bobby had to stay behind to mind the telephone, while his father worked across the yard in the workshops. The Deputy was trying to get his hands on some malleable steel for fabrication and he panicked when Dublin Corporation made an appeal for such material. If they were having difficulties then he would soon be in trouble. He knew of two scrap-metal sources in West Cork. He had already sent Ned Kenny and another man in a truck to Millstreet. And he was expecting a phone-call from a company in Youghal.

The Deputy was also staying put because he expected that the Taoiseach would announce an election in his St Patrick's Day radio broadcast. The Party in rural areas had lobbied the government for a postponement of the election until the danger of invasion and war had passed. A meeting of the local council had passed a resolution calling on the government to postpone the election. But at a meeting in Party HQ in Dublin the Minister for Local Government, Mr MacEntee, said that there would be an election in the spring. And before Christmas, the Minister for Finance, Sean T O'Kelly, said that there would be an election soon and "the sooner we get on with it the better."

So Bobby, like a duty officer, was stuck at home. Except that Alice had volunteered to call on him. Her house call had turned into an offer of looking after the lunch. Now this further development.

The quietness of the house and the music from the wireless and the gramophone combined to lower Bobby's self-control and resistance. It was the first time he had spent so much time alone with her; the effect of this was overpowering. The silence had had an effect on Alice as well: it opened up more than one possibility in her life.

"We must be careful," she said. "We have a duty..."

"It's not wrong to be honest."

"No, but we have obligations to others. You to your family. Your father is a Deputy. And I to my father."

"We're just human, Alice."

"That's not enough. You know about me, Bobby. You know how complicated my life is. Sometimes I want to scream, living here in Cappoquin so far away from the war. Not able to help my father. At least you are able to help your father."

"Things are getting better for your people, Alice. The Russians have the Germans on the run. I read in the *Examiner* that General Golikov's tank and infantry columns have moved westwards. Two thousand Germans surrendered the other day. And look," he took up the day's copy of the paper," the Germans are being captured all around Stalingrad."

Alice placed her hand on his sleeve. "You know that I'm Jewish. You've met my father. The Nazis might still invade Ireland if they were desperate enough. Then everyone with Jewish blood would be rounded up like cattle."

"But nobody knows your religion here. Just my parents and me."

"It's not just religion, it's race, race. The Nazis are too stupid to understand religion. But they've plenty of practice at recognising race."

"I don't understand it, Alice, Asya. Asya, that's the name you were given at birth, isn't it?"

Bobby had longed to use her proper name. He had seen it again recently on a book that she had left behind in the house. It had an exotic resonance for him. It was a mystery. He remembered her father, Mr Schless, using the name in the Glenville office four or five years before. He had overheard a hushed conversation between his father and hers.

"Don't ever use that name!" Alice whispered angrily. "It's death! Death, do you understand?"

"Alice. I'm sorry."

"Your knowing that is a special bond between us." She held his hand. He had small hands, very clean. "It's why we must be careful...with each other."

"I can't stop feeling the way I do. You're beautiful. Every time you come into the house now my heart sinks." He touched her face very lightly. His hand slipped down her neck, without possessiveness or authority, and touched her dress. He could feel her breast, small, rising and falling.

They were silent for a while. Neither of them knew the next move: how to go on or withdraw. It was new territory.

"I love you."

"Don't ever say things like that, Bobby. Don't say that."

"It's the truth. I've loved you since Christmas."

"Only since then!" she said mockingly, trying to regain control.

He took his hand away, annoyed.

They heard shuffling outside the window of the sitting-room. "It must be my father," Bobby said.

"No, it's strangers."

Bobby got up and went to the window. "It's people to meet my father. Last Mass must be over. I suppose I'd better leave them in."

"Dry weather," the first constituent said.

"Great weather," the second one added. Bobby said yes, it was dry weather.

"We need rain badly," a more assertive third man said.

Bobby led them into the sitting-room, which Alice left.

She went into the kitchen. She put the dinner into the fast oven of the stove. Bobby joined her there, but their intimacy had been shattered. Alice didn't seem interested in continuing their conversation. She busied herself at the presses, rooting for glasses and plates. Bobby sat down and stared at the table. It was a different kind of silence, no longer warm.

When the Deputy returned from the yard he went straight into the office that adjoined the sitting-room. He greeted the waiting constituents and hooked one man along with him. The house suddenly took on the atmosphere of a busy doctor's surgery.

"What can I do for you, Jack?" he asked the first constituent, even before the man sat down.

The first two clients merely wanted to sell him scrap metal. Ever since the army manoeuvres of 1942 people had combed the mountains for anything the soldiers had lost or jettisoned: buckles, bullet-cases, buttons, pieces of metal, motor-cycle parts, even helmets. But the Deputy always referred them to Ned Kenny, and reminded them that what had once belonged to the state still belonged to the state.

Other constituents had real problems. An unemployed man told him that he couldn't leave the country because the farmer he had last worked for had registered him as an essential labourer. He had been refused an exit permit. This arrangement suited the farmer, who had registered a number of casual employees and thus forced them to stay put and compete with each other for scarce work. The Deputy promised he'd find out about the man's chances of a permit. He didn't hold out much hope. Another man, with a small farm, had just lost two fields because he failed to comply with a compulsory tillage order. The farmer was wondering if the Deputy could put in a good word for him.

Then a young woman came in. She wanted help in a dispute over butter vouchers. She had bought butter from an unlicensed dealer and wanted to reclaim her vouchers so that she could use them again. "That's a matter for the dealer himself," explained the Deputy. "Listen, I'll have a word with him. I know him." The woman went away smiling.

Later, a shopkeeper who was a staunch supporter of the Party and who employed Ellie's sister, came into the office in an agitated state. He felt insulted that he had been kept waiting. He had been fined fourteen pounds on two counts of having sold tea to unregistered customers. "Money is tight now," he said. "It's not easy. I have two children at boarding-school." The man was small and obese; a born worrier with a violently purple face.

"I'm not sure about this one, Paddy, it's hard to know how to approach it." The Deputy shuffled some papers. He knew—and he knew that the shopkeeper knew—that he couldn't interfere with the judgements of tribunals and courts. But the man was determined not to face the punishment of the courts. He would punish Ellie's sister instead, if the need arose.

"How much time have you got?" asked the Deputy. Then, looking at the man's terrible colour, he added," I mean, to pay this fine."

"Only fifteen days. This government is a pack of Jews and money-grabbers."

"I'd leave the Jews out of it," the Deputy suggested coldly. "They have their own troubles."

"If it wasn't for them this war wouldn't have started in the first place."

"How do you make that out?"

"Well, it was they who started buying and selling nations, bankrupting governments. The Jewish question has been around for hundreds of years."

"I've often worked with Jews," said the Deputy. "I've always found them to be decent fellows. As honest as the day is long..."

"About the fines..." the shopkeeper cut him off.

"I'll have to get advice on this from Dublin. Will you leave it to me? I will write from Dublin, this very week."

"All right, I'll leave it to you." The shopkeeper had visions of the Deputy turning the Department of Justice upside down on his behalf. "Good luck to you, so."

He got up to go. Paudie rose from his chair and walked the man to the door. There were four constituents left.

Finally, at ten minutes to three, the sitting-room was empty. The Deputy headed for the kitchen. A dried-up dinner awaited him. Just then, he noticed an old man hitching an ancient-looking bucket-trap and donkey to the railings. He watched the man through the glass panels of the front door, hoping that he would go away. But he didn't. The old fellow entered through the gate and the Deputy moved disconsolately to greet him.

"Deputy Glenville?" The old man was dressed immaculately in a brown tweed coat and grey woollen scarf. He had a strong voice. "Well, Mr Glenville, it's been a long,

long time."

The Deputy's mind raced. He tried to put a name on the face. He hated forgetting people.

"I know you'll be heading for your dinner, so I'm sorry I'm late. But it's a long trek from Dungarvan." The man looked at him sternly, with authority and directness. His eyes squinted as he took in the Deputy standing before him. "Dear God, you don't know who I am, or, should I say, who I was."

"You have me fooled now."

"You have done very well, by all accounts. You were right to stay in the country. So many others panicked and headed for America when they needn't have. But I always admired your judgement. Always."

Suddenly the Deputy remembered who the old man was.

CHAPTER FIVE

"What did you say to him?" Adele, in her fawn dressing-gown, sorted her clothes for the morning. She had a huge collection of suits and dresses. It had been her practice since her nursing days in America to arrange her outfit before going to bed. The habit had a mildly sedative quality, like reading a light novel. The Deputy was already in bed, propped up by two pillows. He put down a copy of *Rebecca* that he had been toying with since Adele recommended it that afternoon. She was dying to find a convert to Daphne du Maurier. Alice had returned the book to her after complaining that the prose was too "sticky" for her liking. The Deputy looked across the room at his wife, who was now looking at herself in the mirror. She had already said twice that she'd lost weight.

"He was pleading for the life of the IRA man, the one who's been sentenced to death for the killing of the detective in Kilkenny. Several IRA prisoners have gone on hunger-strike. The families have sent hundreds of letters to the newspapers. None has been published, of course, because of the censorship. Frank Aiken and Joe Connolly have really throttled the newspapers."

"The other day Bobby told me that you can't even print the word 'IRA' any more. The newspapers have to call it 'an illegal organisation.'"

"Ah, what does Bobby know?" asked the Deputy. "Anyway, I reminded him that the man had shot a detective. And the officer happens to be related to the minister."

"How did he take that?"

"He asked me how I could be a member of a party that would kill Republicans. How can you live with yourself, says he, a man with your background?" I told him that Dev was dead set against the IRA. Anyone who upsets our neutrality is asking for trouble. Everybody knows that the IRA have been playing around with the Germans." The Deputy pulled the brass chain of his bedside lamp, but the lamp didn't go off. "I must get one of the lads to have a look at that. Come to bed, Adele. You've been wandering around for the last three-quarters of an hour."

Adele climbed into bed reluctantly. She felt very agitated. A day spent at her father's house always unnerved her. "Did the man's family write to the minister and the Taoiseach?"

"They did. Even the old O/C himself wrote."

"Did he get a response?"

"Divil a bit. You see, he wouldn't have much standing with Dev because he made a big song and dance in the papers about refusing an Old IRA pension. Then he had a long article in *The Wolfe Tone Weekly* attacking Dev for facilitating the British during the abdication of Edward VIII. During the abdication crisis Dev summoned the TDs by telegram and had the Dáil pass the Deed of Succession Bill. At the time the British Attorney General praised him for it. I remember that issue of the *Weekly* was banned by Sir Dawson Bates in the Six Counties. Those kinds of thing really annoy Dev."

"He's still an old Republican. He deserves to be listened to."

"Ah, there's a wild streak in those Dungarvan Republicans. They've always been hard to soften. I still get a lot of vicious letters in the Dáil. I got terrible letters when Harte and McGrath were shot on the order of the military court three years ago. One correspondent sent me a ballad. It was written in blood, terrible. Actual blood. That's bitterness for you, depth of feeling. I remember the words of the ballad, what were they now: Patrick McGrath of Dublin and Thomas Harte of Lurgan. Ah, I can't remember...Ah, yes."

"I don't want to hear it," said Adele. "It's just too upsetting."

Because they stood with Emmet, with Tone and with
    Lord Edward,
With the Martyred Three of Manchester and the heroes
    of our day;
Because they fought like true men, the tools of England
    slew them,
And they sleep with Kevin Barry in the lonely prison
    clay.

The Deputy could remember only one stanza. He placed the unread novel on his table. A glass of water was disturbed on its small blue Wedgwood saucer. Drops of liquid fell on to the glass face of his second-best watch.

"Don't wet my Daphne du Maurier," warned Adele.

"Written in blood," he repeated. "Can you imagine such bitterness?"

"I wish you'd told me about those letters. You never tell me these things." Adele was annoyed.

"Why should I worry you? Don't you have enough worries every day, between the children and all the shortages? In another few months we'll all be eating rabbits and grass."

Adele took his right hand and rubbed it vigorously. "Your hands are getting softer," she said. "It's a long time since you did any welding yourself. A long time." She looked at him affectionately, as if he were one of the children. "I have my worries, yes. But it would make me feel more useful if you'd tell me what you're worrying about."

The Deputy put his arm around her. "I told the man that a detective was dead. That's a hanging offence. The cynical IRA officer who sent the young fellow out to shoot the detective is the man who did the dirty business. I know I can appeal to Dev's compassion, I know that. And I will. But I had to tell the man the truth. I don't hold out much hope."

The Deputy took a drink of water. "What really annoyed me," he went on, "was that he got angry. He more or less threatened me."

A look of horror came into Adele's face. "Threaten you?

How could he threaten you? Go to the guards. Don't..."

"Ah, he didn't threaten my life. He knows things about me since the time we were fighting the Free Staters. He said that there were people in the movement now who'd love to expose me."

"Expose you! Expose what?"

"Listen, Adele, there are things from that time that I haven't told anyone. Things about money—where I got it, to buy the forges and the bits of property all around our yard."

"Wasn't it your parents' money?" Adele was as white as a sheet. She spoke in a whisper.

"It was not."

"Oh, God, Paudie. Where did it come from"

"It was IRA money. One of my jobs was to look after the money side of things. I had people from two brigades feeding off my funds."

"Why did you keep this from me? You mean to say that everything we have was built on blood money, cash robbed from banks and post offices?"

"Almost everything I handled came from America. I didn't steal the money," the Deputy explained, agitated. "I suppose you could say I covered its tracks, I hid it. In the early twenties sending volunteers to safe havens like Canada and America was expensive. Boats were often hired to drop volunteers across Lake Ontario into New York State. That cost a lot of money. A good few Irregulars came to me in 1923 without birth certificates or dossiers or military records. Then the American Consular Service changed the regulation about visas—they no longer issued them at Cobh. Everyone was forced to go through Dublin."

"How did the money come into that?"

"I was redundant after the Americans changed the procedures. People in Dublin handled the business. But I still had six hundred pounds hidden away. When I got in touch with the O/C I was told to keep the money. The brigade staff knew that my family had been bombed in Youghal. They figured I'd taken enough punishment."

"You'll have to help the poor boy, so. You can't allow this to come out." Adele spoke with heroic calm.

"That poor boy killed a detective."

"Maybe I should go to see the boy's family. That might help the situation. I could make the family understand your position as a Dáil deputy. They should be told how trapped you are, how boxed-in you are by your position."

"You'll do no such thing!" The Deputy sat upright. He was shocked that Adele would even consider getting involved. "There's no talking to these people. They are fanatics. It'd be easier to change the mind of a bishop."

"I could try. I have an interest in this, you know. My children could be destroyed by propaganda against you."

"We'll see what can be done. The Minister for Justice is a tough one, but I'll talk to him."

"Please do," Adele said earnestly. "Please do."

She turned away from him in bed. Worry spread over her body like a fresh dampness. She felt as if she were sleeping in a wet ditch.

The Deputy put his left arm around her. "Don't worry about it. This is going to be sorted out."

He tightened his embrace around her slim body, but

fell asleep long before her need for love subsided.

CHAPTER SIX

The railway station was a typical stop on the wartime branch line. Employees hurried about, not because they were busy, but because they needed to create the illusion of busyness. A young railway clerk was eyeing the Deputy's daughter furtively. A small piebald donkey cropped the last harvest of daffodils along the rhododendron hedge that was the pride and joy of the station-master. Chrissie didn't feel like raising her head to shoo away the animal; a north-easterly breeze was blowing. She eyed the clerk occasionally, and wondered what he was thinking about. He was a quiet man.

Chrissie looked up the line in the Waterford direction. There was a goods shed with sliding doors that opened on to a railway siding with steel buffers. She could see a truck from O'Connor's farm laden with skinned and gutted rabbits for England. She could hear, coming from behind her, the slow grind of Watson's truck that was laden with salmon and butter for the war market. Ireland was neutral but almost everything it produced seemed destined for Allied warehouses.

Down the line, in the Lismore direction, the gates of the level-crossing were opened. And five minutes later, the first murmur of a train.

"It's late," Ned Kenny said. He had grown tired of waiting in the car. He placed himself in front of Chrissie, and leaned forward to watch the approaching train. His presence annoyed Chrissie.

"You go back to the car," she said. "Anyway, I don't know why you need the car. Dada always walks home. Why don't you take the car back to the yard?"

"He might have heavy cases. He might have election material. You'd never know." Ned was holding his ground. He looked forward to the Deputy's homecomings like a son.

"Go back, Ned. Wait in the car. I insist." There was a ferocious look on Chrissie's face.

"I'll stay." Ned stretched himself to his full length, which made him momentarily taller than Chrissie. But he was afraid to look at her. He couldn't bear her look of disapproval.

"I insist," she repeated.

This time Ned knew that he had no chance. He was afraid that Chrissie would say something to her father. She would make something up, some wounding incident, just to undermine the Deputy's high opinion of him. He didn't trust her an inch. He went back to the car and slammed the heavy door. Chrissie resumed her lonely vigil. The train arrived. Her father was already standing at the door, ready to step down. She ran to the green carriage but Mr Kelleher, the station-master, got there before her.

"A busy week then?" he said as he took the Deputy's document-case.

"It's all go now. But I had to come back for that funeral," the Deputy replied as he stepped off the train. Only two others got off, both British soldiers in mufti, home on leave before they returned to the staff college at Camberly. One of them deliberately brushed against Chrissie and she snarled at him.

"Chrissie, love." Her father's face brightened as he handed her his battered leather case. He held on to the heavy suitcase. They hugged. "Where's Ned? How are your mother's headaches? Bobby said on the phone that her migraines were coming back."

"They're not serious," Chrissie reassured him. She led him from the platform. "When will the election be? You look tired, Dada."

He didn't hear her. "How's school going?" he asked.

"Dada, I've outgrown it."

"Don't give up on it yet."

The Deputy had come home in mid-session to attend the funeral of Mrs Villiers-Stuart, a Catholic Anglo-Irishwoman who had been involved in the local Red Cross Society. He intended to stay home until Easter to organise the Party and to attend the consecration of the new Bishop of Waterford and Lismore, Dr Cahalane. He would miss the second reading of the General Elections (Emergency Provisions) Bill, which had been moved in the Dáil by the Minister for Local Government.

"Where the hell is Ned?"

"He's in the car."

"And he left you standing out here in the cold!"

"I told him to stay away. You're my father, not his, for God's sake."

"What did they say when you said you'd miss the second reading of the bill?" Ned asked him when he got into the car. But before the Deputy could reply he was bombarded with further questions—about the fined shopkeeper, the plight of agricultural labourers, the petrol supply, and the timing of the next election. The Deputy began at the beginning: "Ah, that's all sorted out; half the Dáil will be at Dr Cahalane's consecration."

"And the IRA man, any movement at all?"

"Nothing doing. I've no reply so far from the Minister for Justice. Counsel for the condemned lad is trying everything in the courts. A lot of the deputies are sorry for the poor young fellow. It's the leaders of the IRA who should know better. We're in a serious situation with the war."

"If they execute the lad there'll be trouble." Ned sounded angry.

"There would be worse trouble if the British had a pretext for the invasion of Ireland. The IRA siding with the Germans has put us all in danger. I'm telling you, they don't realise what danger they've put us all into."

Chrissie had lapsed into a sulky silence.

⋅⋆⋅

Two days later the Deputy attended Mrs Villiers-Stuart's funeral. Ned and Bobby and a professor from Mount

Melleray College shared his car. The funeral was a silent and moving affair; few cars, but hundreds of ponies and traps. A guard of honour was formed by the local Red Cross, with Adele marching in front in Red Cross uniform. Members of the Local Security Force carried the coffin for the entire one and a half miles to the graveyard through dense estate woodland. The dead aristocrat had been a good employer who protected her flock of tenants with her own personal wealth. Almost all the members of the LSF had been her employees, so the grief on their faces was real and personal. The Deputy wondered how many of their names would be added to the list of the unemployed.

That evening Ned and the Deputy went over the sales and supply books of the business. In the short term things looked good. They had enough fuel to keep them in business for three months, and they had made a good margin on scrap-metal deals. While they were talking together Bobby came into the workshop. He watched them for a while and realised that the atmosphere was good. This gave him enough courage to ask his father for a half-gallon of petrol. It wasn't right, he said, to have two motor-bikes idle for so long; the parts might rust, the blocks might seize up.

"I don't have fuel for pleasure. You know that. There's an emergency on." His father was annoyed to be asked.

"Just half a gallon. You have a full supply tank. Even the reserve tank in the backyard is full."

"And do you know why?" his father continued. "Because we've been careful."

Ned was sorry for Bobby. He didn't want to witness his embarrassment either. "Maybe two pints, what do you think, Deputy?"

The Deputy sighed, then clicked his tongue. He threw his indelible pencil on to a workbench in a gesture of exasperation. "Sure, sure, boy. But just two pints. And take it from the tank in the backyard."

"Ah, good man!" Bobby was thrilled.

"Don't ride up and down Main Street, for God's sake. There's an election coming up. I don't want local councillors saying my child is wasting valuable fuel. Go down to the 'bank.'"

Bobby ran off across the yard.

"He's delighted with himself," Ned noted, pleased.

"He's a wild bloody child."

"He's a man now."

"He has a dangerous, reckless streak. It doesn't come from my side of the family. All my family were timid carpenters. Maybe we should have put him to work with a carpenter. Woodwork is a great sedative, so it is." The Deputy shoved the red sales book and ledger into their pigeon-holes and looked through the large office window. He watched his son carrying a milk bottle full of petrol. The look of delight on Bobby's face filled him with a sudden pleasure. "Ah, God," he sighed.

"What's the matter?" asked Ned.

"I was thinking there of the young IRA lad. He never had much. And his poor family. There's enough killing in the world without the government adding to it."

"I do think about him too."

"You know, not a day goes by now without my thinking of him. I hate to think of him being hanged."

ASYA AND CHRISTINE

"His poor mother," added Ned.

"And his comrades, his cracked misguided comrades. If he's hanged they'll feel like martyrs. They'll just stop thinking altogether."

"My father still talks about the murder of Erskine Childers by the Cosgrave government. Hanging people just adds to the anger."

"I'm doing my best," the Deputy said. "I really am doing my best. We can't be hanging people in an election year."

Ned suggested that the Deputy write to the papers. Put pressure on Dev. The Deputy couldn't believe this; he couldn't believe that Ned could be so reckless.

"Mrs Glenville did her bit anyway. The man's family wasn't a bit hostile. She expected trouble."

"What do you mean, Ned?" The Deputy looked at him, horror mounting in his face.

"I'm sure she was going to tell you. Didn't she tell you?" Ned was terrified.

"When, when the hell did this happen?"

"Last Wednesday."

"Why didn't you phone me on Wednesday, for Christ's sake?"

"Mrs Glenville said she'd told you she was going to do it."

"Jesus Christ!" The Deputy, swearing, bolted out of the office.

[75]

CHAPTER SEVEN

The Deputy was furious. How could she be so stupid, how could she, how could she, he kept repeating to himself as he barged into the house. Adele was in the kitchen, watching the lone blackbird that came to the window to feed on breadcrumbs. The afternoon light was unkind to her, revealing tiny lines near her mouth and exaggerating the tiredness of the skin around her eyes. She had just come out of another migraine attack. "It's getting cold out there," she said absentmindedly. Gerald and Emer were still at the kitchen table doing schoolwork. The others were in the dining-room, where the fire burned already and the tea-table was set. The fire was always lit in the dining-room when their father was home.

"Adele, did you see that IRA man's family?"

"Of course I did. Didn't I say I would?" Adele was unmoved by his tone. "Where's Bobby?" she asked. "It's nearly tea-time, everything is ready."

The Deputy was momentarily distracted. "We gave him a pint of petrol for his machine."

"What! At a time when the rest of the country has to

walk! Isn't that irresponsible, now, isn't it?"

"Why did you go to see these people?"

"I told you I would go, love. You should know by now that when I say I'll do something I mean it."

"And who else was there? Who saw you there? That place is crawling with Special Branch men."

"What do I care? I wasn't committing a crime."

"You were offering support. They thrive on that kind of thing. I haven't even met the minister yet. Now he'll have a report on your visit before I even get to see him."

"What of it?" She dismissed his concern and his anger completely. "For goodness sake, Paudie, you are a Dáil deputy. I am entitled to report on things for you. I have a legitimate interest. The condemned man is your constituent. His poor mother is your constituent. They deserve our interest, if not our comfort. What's wrong with you?"

"I'm just shocked that you would do this without telling me. You have never interfered in my constituency work before."

"Interfere! How dare you use that word to me!" she shouted angrily, flinging a tea-towel on to the draining-board. "I'm not interfering. I'm helping. Most of your fellow deputies are too bloody cowardly to go near this family. If you'd only stop being indignant for a moment, I could tell you what it's like in that house!"

The children, frightened by their raised voices, fled to the refuge of the dining-room. The whole house had its ears pricked, scared, not knowing what to expect. This was new territory. Their parents had bantered and teased each other before but this was different. They heard Adele's angry voice, fearless and full of authority. "Close that door and sit down!"

The Deputy did as he was told, muttering something about his disappointment.

"What are you saying?" Adele went on. "I am trying to help. If your name is blackened all of us will be hurt. You would have to withdraw as a Party candidate. Think of the embarrassment!"

"I do think of it, woman," the Deputy shouted. "It's the very thing that worries me all the time. But these people are best avoided until I talk to the minister involved. It's a serious business."

"You needn't tell me how serious it is! The child's mother is in agony. Her son will be hanged. How will she cope with that?" She went over to the stove and checked something in the top oven. She removed a dish. "This is burning," she said angrily. "You should see the poverty in that house; those people have nothing. They can't even get jobs as casual labourers. Before the relief money falls due each week the boy's mother and sister starve. They don't eat, they just stay in bed. Does Mr Dev have to stay in bed, answer me that? I called to their house on Wednesday evening. They had a bit of bread left, but after that was eaten they wouldn't have a thing until Friday. They are crazy with hunger. It's hunger that makes them desperate. And then there's the authorities."

"The authorities do their best..."

"Their best! They persecute them night and day. Guards and plain-clothes men knocking on the door at all times of day and night; turning their pathetic bedding upside down, breaking furniture, abusing them. Dear Jesus, what can a poor mother know?"

"Look, the guards have to investigate. Young women are constantly being used as couriers. Wasn't a girl from Carrick blown sky-high while carrying explosives before Christmas? You can be sure that was destined for use against the guards or the prison wardens."

"The house is watched constantly. They know damn well there is nothing inside."

"The lad murdered a detective-sergeant," the Deputy reminded her. "Don't allow your feelings to blind you. These people are really dangerous. If it weren't for the brilliance of Dev these people would have had the country embroiled in the war long before now. Think of the thousands of Irish children that would be killed in those air-raids that we read about. Do you think the Germans or the Allies would give two hoots for the Irish if it came to a head? You can be sure that either side would destroy the country. The Allies have even bombed Paris because it's in their military interest. Half the French people are fighting against Hitler yet the Allies bombed the capital of France. That's the reality of the war. Neutrality is the only weapon we possess. Our own army has the strength of only one or two divisions. When the Germans moved westwards they wiped out over a hundred divisions."

"What's that got to do with a boy dying in prison?"

"Everything! You mustn't let your feelings get in the way of thinking. These Republicans would align us with German interests because of their hatred of England. They would drive us into the war and we'd be annihilated."

"So the child must hang and the family must starve every week for the rest of its days."

"They are dangerous people. And remember, I was threatened."

"I told the mother that you were going to speak to the minister. She was full of hope when I left."

"You shouldn't have given her any hope."

"And why not? She has little else. The boy won't be hanged for at least three months. Let her live in hope for three months."

"Foolish, foolish. Don't be offering hope where there's no hope." The Deputy looked at her directly now. His anger had subsided, though not completely.

"But you haven't even spoken to the minister yet."

"Don't pin any hopes on that meeting."

"They have no leaders," Adele said. "All their natural leaders are in prison or gone away. They really need someone to speak for them... You always said that the best leaders of the Republicans were sent away to America."

"It is true. We sent some of the brainiest away."

"I wonder what's keeping Bobby?" Adele said, switching the conversation. They hadn't decided on a plan of action. He hadn't withdrawn his accusation of foolishness. She hadn't felt any repentance.

"He won't come back until he runs out of petrol. You can be sure of that."

"Well, he'll have to be happy with something cold. We're going to eat this now. It's already burned." She put her hands on her hips in an uncharacteristic matronly gesture. The Deputy picked up *The Times Tutorial* and left the kitchen. In the living-room the girls were discussing Lieutenant Kiely yet again.

"He asked me a lot of questions, about you. He was very curious," said Emer.

"What? What did he want to know?" Chrissie begged.

"I won't tell you."

"You rotten bitch!"

"None of that talk in this house," said the Deputy.

Adele came through the door, carrying a shepherd's pie on top of five hot plates. "Will someone help me," she shouted.

Emer said, "I think he's a snob. I heard the girls in Kerfoots saying that he was a snob."

"Well, if he's a snob, he must have something to be snobbish about. What is it, I wonder?" asked the Deputy.

"He's a great dancer," Chrissie explained.

"That's not going to get him through life," her father said.

"It's a help," said Adele.

"Where's Alice?" the Deputy asked suddenly. "She's usually with us at this time of day."

"She's above in the house," Chrissie replied. "Mrs Heaphy and herself started to paint the kitchen chairs. Isn't that incredible?"

The Deputy picked at his pie. "It's not good for her to be alone, not good at all." He was worried about Alice. He had received a letter from her father in Bradford, who had recently met a man who had escaped from Germany through Denmark and Sweden. The man had told him horrific stories; how all his friends had been picked up and had disappeared. "I would rather my daughter die than fall into the hands of these monsters," Mr Schless had written. The Deputy had replied to him by return, reassuring him that Alice was safe. Yet he felt deeply for the father's position, away from his daughter and with a submarine-infested sea between them.

"You haven't touched your pie." Adele pointed at his plate.

"I'm not that hungry. We had a big lunch."

Then the doorbell rang. The Deputy got up quickly. "It's probably Ned Kenny."

But when he opened the door he found Bobby. "Jesus, boy, what have you done to yourself?" Bobby had fallen off his bike. His face was disfigured by grease-marks and shallow, bleeding wounds. His upper lip was swollen. He was holding his left elbow and grimaced with pain. His trouser-leg was torn, and through the gaping cloth the Deputy could see Bobby's raw bleeding knee.

"Your mother will clean you up," the Deputy said, leading him through the hallway.

Adele gasped when she saw her son. "Where did this happen?"

"On the railway bank. The machine bucked and came over on top of me."

"You'll have to get to the bathroom. Can you climb the stairs?"

"Yes, my leg is fine."

"Did you leave the BSA on the railway line?" his father asked.

"Mr Kelleher put it into the goods shed."

In the bathroom Adele dabbed his knee with strips of cloth soaked in gentian violet. Emer, her face screwed up in disgust, wiped the grease from his face. "At least your eyes weren't touched," she said.

His elbow hurt. "I think Dr White should see that," Adele said. "Change your trousers before he sees you."

Bobby didn't want the fuss. He felt embarrassed. They went downstairs to wait for the doctor. Bobby begged them for a cup of tea, but Adele wouldn't allow him to have anything until the doctor had seen him.

CHAPTER EIGHT

"I suppose there's more to a man than looks," said Chrissie.

Ellie didn't agree. "Don't be daft, girl. A man is an open book. You can tell nearly everything by looking into his face."

Chrissie raised herself on to the topmost step of the entrance to Ryan's Drapers Store so that she could see her Lieutenant Kiely marching past. It was the Easter parade, made up of regular soldiers and the geriatric throng of the LSF.

"I really don't like uniforms," admitted Alice. "But he is handsome in his uniform. He certainly is."

"I wonder if he's a Protestant?" asked Ellie.

"How could he be a Protestant. Hasn't he just come out of Mass?" Chrissie replied, annoyed. "Anyway, I don't care if he's the wrong religion. I'm interested only in him." She didn't want her desire to be weakened by wretched details. "He has such sensitive eyes," she went on. "Sometimes he seems to be on the point of tears. There's a lot of sadness there."

The others said nothing. Then, after a while, Ellie piped

up, "Did ye hear about Mr Mellerick and what happened yesterday?"

"What happened?" asked Alice.

"Ned, the tailor, was working at his window when he thought he saw leaves falling to the ground outside. He thought they were leaves from the big sycamore."

"Sure, that's been cut down," Chrissie said.

"I know...But Ned says it looked like a big shower of leaves. It was only when one settled on his window-sill that he realised that they weren't leaves at all."

"What were they?"

"Money! Big five-pound notes. Ned nearly fell off his chair with the fright. He jumped up and went outside. It was raining money. Ned and Noel found the path and the gutter full of tenners, fivers and pound notes. It was Noel who pointed to the window of Mellerick's loft. They could see Mr Mellerick's boy at the window pushing rolled-up cash through a gap in the sash. Ned was disgusted. He thought the money was coming from heaven."

"Did he really?" Alice asked.

"That's Ned's story, anyway. He gathered up four hundred and fifty pounds. Ned said that at least another hundred pounds must have blown against a group of the Children of Mary who were coming from a church meeting. Of course that money was never seen again."

"What a wonderful story," said Alice.

"I don't believe a word of it," said Chrissie.

"Mr Mellerick nearly killed his son. The boy won't be able to sit down for a week," Ellie insisted.

"It is a wonderful story. Ned Lonergan tells great stories

always."

"Jesus, look at the time!" Ellie screamed suddenly. "Your mother will kill me, Chrissie. I'm supposed to put on the dinner."

"Don't worry about it. We'll all go home now."

The town square was filled with people now that the military had passed by. Cloth-capped men, stooping women, badly clothed children, all moved forward and planned their next stop. Crowds of tired men pushed their way into the pubs, Coppertorns, Kennys, The Central Bar.

ૐ

In Dublin the government and the opposition parties were preoccupied with the budget. A white paper was published that revealed a shortfall of nearly five million pounds. People were worried in case this would mean an increase in income-tax. There was also a severe potato shortage: a "famine" the opposition deputies called it in an effort to arouse emotion. The Minister for Supplies rejected all criticism, reminding them that there was plenty of bread and flour in the country. The people wouldn't starve, and he implied that anyone who made the general public feel that they *would* starve was unpatriotic.

The newspapers were full of news from the war in the world outside: the collapse of German divisions in North Africa, the capture of Bizerta and Tunis, huge Allied bombing raids on Europe; the bombing of The Hague and the railway yards at Abbéville and Antwerp. At the time, the RAF made spectacular hits against the dams of the Mohne and Sorpe, which controlled two-thirds of the water-storage capacity of the Ruhr Basin. Railways, power stations, villages and homes had been washed away by millions of tons of water. It was a spectacular propaganda coup for the British. Even in so-called neutral Dublin the public hungrily consumed the details of the raids.

꙰

On Budget Day, 5 May, the Deputy walked from his room to the Dáil. He was too preoccupied to notice the crispness of the morning or the pair of early swallows that dived low over the canal. In his bag he carried a letter from the Minister for Justice, as well as the morning copy of the *Cork Examiner*, the only newspaper to carry news from the southern constituencies. The minister's letter was friendly and full of promise. He had addressed him by his first name—A Phaudie, a chara—and had gone on to praise his work and the compassion he had shown for the condemned man's family. It would be a sad thing for the son of any Irish mother to die by hanging, the minister added, especially since the hangman would have to be imported from England. But he had no real power in the matter. Whether the man would hang or not was a matter for the Taoiseach. These things came up in cabinet, but unless Dev had doubts on the issue it was a waste of time to raise it at a cabinet meeting. But (and this is what filled the Deputy with hope) he, the minister, was of the personal opinion that Dev didn't want the blood of yet another IRA youth on his hands.

This contradicted what the Deputy had been told by his fellow backbenchers. He decided there and then to meet the Taoiseach's secretary, to seek a meeting with the Chief himself. The minister had agreed to speak with the relevant authorities about the alleged harassment of the man's family. The minister had that within his power. At least that was something.

But it was difficult to set up a meeting. The government was preoccupied with finance and with the problem of setting an opportune date for the election. But a life was at stake: this impelled the Deputy to action. The minister had written that he had sent a copy of the Deputy's letter to the Taoiseach's office. The Deputy could see, in his mind's eye, a friendly meeting with Dev, a moment of triumph in the inner sanctum.

By the time he reached Kildare Street he was exhausted. He bumped into Peadar O'Donnell, the once-radical Republican, as they turned in the gate of the Dáil. He and the Deputy had had lunch together in February of 1942 when O'Donnell had been appointed temporary labour adviser to the government.

"More tax, I suppose, Deputy?" the soft-voiced Donegal-man remarked.

"Looks like it, Peadar."

"The whole country is broke."

"Look at it this way," the Deputy said, thinking of the morning's headlines," at least the RAF isn't flying against us!"

"Not yet anyway," O'Donnell joked.

Inside the house the budget was a damp squib. In the

sluggish fiscal atmosphere of the Emergency there could be little change or improvement. And there was none. The standard rate of income-tax was held at seven and sixpence in the pound. But the minister's introductory remarks were caustic. In the demands coming from all quarters, he said there was evidence of a sort of financial hysteria. He blamed the bad example set by the belligerents in the present world conflict. That evening, after several boring hours of budget discussion, the Deputy returned to his quarters. There was a note on his table telling him that his wife had rung. He was to phone her as soon as possible. He immediately picked up the handset and rang the operator.

Adele answered. "I thought you'd never phone."

"What is it?"

"It's poor Ellie. She collapsed this morning. She was sweeping the sitting-room. I put her to bed and called Dr White."

"How is she?"

"You know, she had a terrible cough for weeks. Chrissie was at her all the time to go and see a doctor. She coughed up some blood."

"We'd better prepare for the worst."

Adele explained that the doctor had taken blood and mucus samples. They could do tests in the county clinic. The doctor was worried by her swollen glands. "We'll have to look after Ellie like a daughter," said the Deputy. "We'll not send her back to her own place, or let them put her into a hospital."

"She knows that."

"You tell her again. You tell her that we'll look after

her." He was sorry for Ellie. She had been riding the crest of a wave since her engagement to young Kavanagh. There had been little joy in her life, apart from the recent triumph of becoming a fiancée. Ellie had been born into a family of weak men. It was the women—Ellie and her two sisters—who had gone out into the world and sought employment. Her father and her brothers were still at home, moaning about the lack of good work, the meanness of farmers and the shortage of good poaching. They did nothing to make the lives of the womenfolk any easier. That was a common enough pattern among the rural working class: this cowardice and moral defeatism of the men. Only the women couldn't afford to give up: they would support entire families on the pittance earned as domestics or shop-assistants. When the Deputy said, "We'll look after Ellie," he really meant it.

"And," Adele said, turning away from the alarms of Ellie, "you'll never guess what our brave Chrissie has been up to."

From the tone of her voice the Deputy could tell that it was nothing life-threatening.

"She's got herself invited to *Rose Marie* at the Cork Opera House. Young Lieutenant Kiely walked straight up to her after the explosives demonstration in Lismore and asked her out."

"The explosions must have gone to his head," the Deputy laughed.

"True. I could never imagine him being so audacious. He seems such a timid creature. Not at all right for Chrissie."

"Aren't you jumping the gun a bit?" The Deputy teased

her. "But this is a very big thing for Chrissie. She's only a schoolgirl."

"Don't talk to me. We've had terrible fights all this week. She wants to give up school."

"And do what?"

"Help at home."

"Over my dead body. Tell her she's to finish her school year."

"Don't I keep telling her," Adele replied, exasperated. "Don't I just keep telling her!"

But Adele returned to the subject of the lieutenant. He was going to Cork with a party of officers and their wives. He had promised Chrissie that they would get home by twelve-thirty. Chrissie told him quite coolly that she would have to think about it. But when she told her mother she couldn't conceal her joy: "He's asked me! He's asked me!" she kept repeating.

The Deputy, hanging on to the phone in Dublin, felt at a remove from all this excitement. He was still trying to come to terms with the worrying news about Ellie. Obviously, Adele was using the joy of Chrissie's excitement as a counterweight to Ellie's illness.

"I don't know if she should be allowed to go all the way to Cork with a busload of men. She might be given drink or something."

"The wives are going with the men. It will be all couples."

The doorbell rang in the Deputy's hallway. The caller was Senator Goulding, a colleague, up from Lismore to discuss the coming county convention with the Minister for Posts and Telegraphs. The three of them would be part of the panel. "Go on inside," the Deputy motioned him towards the sitting-room.

"Is there anything else?" he asked his wife.

"Oh, Healy's shop in Lismore was destroyed by fire. A huge fire, three engines. You should write a short note to them."

"I'll do that."

CHAPTER NINE

When the Deputy entered Ellie's room he was filled with disgust. The blinds were partially drawn, making the room bleak and sinister. A pathetic Sacred Heart lamp burned in the corner. Its very presence seemed an invitation to death. The room smelled of Jeyes Fluid and carbolic soap. Ellie was dozing. The Deputy tapped her pale white arm and she was startled into waking.

"Mr Glenville?"

"Ellie, who put you into this prison-camp?" He smiled down at her.

She turned to the darkened windows. "Mrs Glenville says everything must be spotless. There's a lot of lorries going down the street on their way to the station."

"Nonsense, Ellie. You'll enjoy listening to the lads from O'Connor's factory." He went across the room and pulled the curtains back fully and opened the window.

"The breeze is cold."

"You're right," he admitted and closed the window again.

"Will you open it for me in the morning?"

"I will surely, girl. The smell of that carbolic would flatten a horse. Has your Michael been visiting?"

"He has not," Ellie replied. "He has too much respect for me. You can be sure the people of the town would be gossiping if they thought he was visiting me in a bedroom."

"Who the hell cares about gossip! Aren't ye going to be married?"

"If I don't die first."

"You're not going to die at all. Hasn't Adele told you that you haven't real consumption at all? It's only a glandular fever thing? Haven't they told you that?"

"I don't believe Dr White at all. I'm not going to get better."

"More fresh air!" exclaimed the Deputy. "And we'll have to drag young Kavanagh in to see you. If he's a man at all he'll jump in there beside you."

"Mr Glenville!"

When he went back downstairs, Adele was waiting for his verdict. "Well, what do you think?"

"She's grand, isn't she? I don't know what all the fuss was about. Her room looks like a mortuary."

"I didn't want the dust from the street coming in," Adele explained.

"We should get Bobby to haul in young Kavanagh."

"Ellie's afraid of people talking."

"Ah, never mind people talking. Kavanagh's the best medicine she could get. What harm anyway if he hops into bed with her. Doesn't the girl deserve a bit of fun?"

"This is a Christian house, Paudie."

"Ah, life is too short for petty worries." He sat down

and picked up a paper. He was unhappy. He couldn't put his finger on it, but something wasn't right. Sometimes he felt like a stranger in his own home. His long absences in Dublin were turning him into a loner, an outsider. The atmosphere in the house wasn't good.

"Did you get the part for Mr Hickey?" Adele asked.

"Part?"

"He called yesterday. He said you promised to look for a clip or something for his projector."

"Oh, Christ!" He had forgotten. Mr Hickey was the local cinema owner. He was finding it difficult to survive the war. It was impossible to import new projection equipment, and even the print quality of films was deteriorating. In the thirties Mr Hickey was a happy man. Then, people used to say that owning a cinema was a licence to print money. But not any more. Fuel was scarce. Spares were impossible to come by and Mr Hickey wore a frightened look. The Deputy had let him down. "I forgot to look for that bloody pin. I wouldn't mind but he sent a letter up to the Dáil with the addresses of two suppliers."

"You'd better phone him."

"I will! I will!"

The next day, when the Deputy and a Party worker called to Ned Kenny's house to give him a lift to the selection convention in Dungarvan, he wasn't there. His brother explained that he had left earlier that day on a bicycle. He said he'd see them there. "Why would a man cycle eleven miles when he knows that he could have a lift?" the Deputy asked.

"I know what's wrong with that fellow," Tom Lincoln said.

"I hope you do. What is it?"

"Woman trouble. He's been seeing a girl out in Boreenatra."

"That's where the IRA lad's family lives," the Deputy said.

"Well, this one's a nice girl. Her father was a great hurler. I often watched him playing in Fraher's field."

"By God, he must be very enthusiastic. Mind you, 'tis hard to imagine Ned cycling towards a bit of romance."

Tom Lincoln laughed.

When they arrived at the hotel Ned was already there, standing under a large deer's head, talking to Paddy Little, the Minister for Posts and Telegraphs. "Have you been here long?" asked Tom Lincoln.

"Over an hour. You're late. Anyway, everything is in order. Everything will go as arranged."

They walked into the hall together. The Deputy and the minister moved up to the platform behind the podium because they were part of the panel of candidates. Within an hour, with no tension, without ceremony and without debate, the candidates for the election were ratified. Then Sean T O'Kelly, the Minister for Finance, stood up and addressed the crowd. He gave an exciting and rousing speech; more Republican in tone than any speech that the Deputy had heard from a Fianna Fáil politician since the outbreak of the war. Maybe the minister had cut his speech to suit the town of Dungarvan, always a Republican place. O'Kelly was forceful in his comments: "We have something to be proud of," he shouted," because we are the lineal descendants of Sinn Féin and we've taken the torch from them to carry on the fight for freedom."

The delegates were inspired by this and cheered loudly. The Deputy couldn't help thinking about the IRA man's family, and the misguided people who thought that the current IRA struggle was a legitimate thing.

"Isn't it a grand speech?" Mr Little turned to the Deputy.

"Certainly better than the budget speech," the Deputy replied.

"Do I detect a note of sarcasm?"

"Not at all. At least we know where we stand on the national question. It gets very confusing at times."

He looked across at the minister, who was now being mobbed by the delegates. Tom Lincoln came up to the Deputy and said," You should get a move on. The IRA man's family. You should go now."

"What!" exclaimed Mr Little.

"The Republican who's been sentenced to hang. I promised that I'd visit his family today. That's in order, isn't it?"

"I wouldn't get too close to these people," Mr Little said. "I do feel sorry for their families, you know that...But we find ourselves in an election campaign. They always make things awkward for the Party."

"It's only the lad's mother."

"I see."

"She's not a candidate!" Tom Lincoln joked. But the minister didn't see the humour in it.

The Deputy moved on. After leaving the hotel he drove

to the row of labourers' cottages. At the entrance to the
row he was stopped by the old O/C, the man who had
visited him on St Patrick's Day. He was still wearing the
rough tweeds. He seemed very nervous, looking over his
shoulder, as if he expected to be picked up by the guards.

When they arrived at the IRA man's house the old man
pushed the door open in a familiar way. "It's us, Kit!" he
shouted. "It's the Deputy!"

They were met and acknowledged without enthusiasm
by a woman in her early sixties. Her skin was sallow, and
there were deep furrows in her forehead. She wore a filthy
linen apron of traditional blue-and-white stripes.

"In here," she said.

When they stepped inside he saw three younger people,
two men and a woman. The girl was very beautiful, with
black hair in long tight plaits. She smiled. The two young
men looked at the Deputy with savage hostility. They were
unshaven and badly dressed. Both had bits of twine instead
of laces in their boots. There were no introductions so the
Deputy never learned the names of the children. They were
props; somehow they amplified the mother's suffering.

"How can they kill my child?" The mother spoke
suddenly, articulate with anger, her voice tiny.

The old man tried to calm her. "Don't be upset, Kit.
Hear what the Deputy has to say."

"They're all traitors to Ireland, those TDs."

"The Deputy is worried about you..."

"He's the only one that's worried, then."

"Have the guards left you alone?" asked the Deputy.

"Have they what! My two sons can't get jobs. They've

searched our house twice these last weeks. They tear up the mattresses and cut the bits of furniture we have. They even abuse my daughter."

"I'm going to meet Dev himself, Mrs Fahey," the Deputy said. "I promise I'll do everything. I won't stop till I have persuaded Dev."

"The sentence could be commuted," the old man suggested.

The mother sat down beside her daughter. Life imprisonment was a straw she could clutch at. There was nothing else. Public opinion was controlled by the government through censorship. Her three children, the dishevelled and the beautiful, listened impassively.

The Deputy suddenly noticed that the bench they were sitting on was the frame, the skeleton, of a couch. It had been ripped apart so often that the family had removed the chintz covering and the stuffing. It meant less of a cleaning-up job after a police raid.

"This is terrible, Mrs Fahey," he said. He was thinking of the couch, but the mother thought he meant her son. Her daughter looked at him. There was such a look of defeat in her eyes. It was years since he had seen that look on a young face. It wasn't good.

"I'll be speaking to Dev himself," the Deputy repeated.

"I have a letter for him," the mother said. She stood up to fetch it.

CHAPTER TEN

The Deputy wasn't sorry when the business of the tenth Dáil ended on Wednesday, 28 May. He hadn't contributed one word to a parliamentary debate. As he walked back to his house he regretted not having made one or two interjections just to get into the records. It had been a difficult Dáil for all the backbench deputies. Because of the shortage of newsprint, only the ministers and opposition spokesmen—those who handled the main issues of the Emergency—were given any exposure. A backbench TD would have had to commit suicide in the Dáil chamber to get any publicity. Still, the Deputy had done a vast amount of constituency work since 1938. His representations on behalf of social assistance recipients, small farmers, cornered businessmen, TB patients, tax-evaders and inshore fishermen had run into thousands. He was confident of re-election.

Earlier in the week he had run into Paddy Little, the minister who was his constituency colleague. Little was a strange man, an exotic bird within the Party. He had been a TD for Waterford since 1927, and before that editor of *New Ireland* and *An Phoblacht*. Between 1933 and 1939 he was Dev's parliamentary secretary. His father had been Prime Minister of Newfoundland.

"You look down-hearted, Deputy," Mr Little said. "Did you get my note?"

"What note?"

"On your desk. I had it delivered to your desk."

"Is it about the condemned lad?"

"Yes! Dev says he's willing to have a chat with you. At a convenient time. He has to leave for Carlow, a big election rally. You are homeward bound yourself?"

"I am. But I could hold on here in Dublin for a day or two."

"No point. Dev's movements are too complicated for the rest of the week. Go home to Cappoquin."

"We must save that man's life, Paddy."

"And we shall. But you know how hostile the Chief is to the IRA. If they had their way we'd all be involved in this appalling war in Europe."

"A life is a life. Even a bad life."

"Don't get too deeply involved in this. I've seen men's political careers destroyed because they became obsessed with one issue. You have to have a balance. You owe it to the people who voted for you."

A sudden blast of wind caught them unawares. As the minister's right hand shot up to retrieve his hat, some of the papers he was carrying fell to the ground. The two men stooped to retreive them. The papers were carbon copies of poems. "My brother's poems," the minister said, slightly embarrassed. "Philip Francis. I'm writing a foreword to his collection. He died the year before I entered the Dáil."

"I heard that he was a great sailor."

"Yes, yes, he was," Mr Little smiled. "When I was a child he sailed around the world in an old windjammer. When he was in his twenties he sailed to Australia twice, first in the *Hesperus*, then in the *Pericles*. But he was a mystic as well. He had a wonderful imagination."

"A long way from politics."

"Not entirely unconnected. He felt for the national struggle. He liked to compare our struggle to that of the Greeks: a small country's ultimate victory over superior forces. But he wasn't a man of action."

"I'll go and get your note," the Deputy said. "The note," he repeated. The minister was lost in a personal reverie.

"Ah, yes, the note. Don't be depressed, Deputy. There is hope. All is not lost." He tidied the bundle of his dead brother's poems, reverently. "But our first priority is the election."

"I need to be sure that I've done everything I can."

"I don't understand."

"For the young IRA man. I need to be satisfied that I've done everything."

"But it is important not to get too deeply implicated in the matter. Not in this election year. A government that loses power has no power, and can't save anyone. There's no great mysticism in that." These were Paddy Little's parting remarks.

The Deputy left Dublin on the following day. As usual, the journey southwards was slow and boring. He was delayed even longer than usual by an accident involving a passenger train on the Waterford line. He was joined in his carriage by Sir John Keane, the southern Unionist senator, an outspoken critic of government policies. Sir John was a West Waterford farmer as well as a banker. In fact the Deputy was Sir John's tenant because he held his forges under a long lease from the Keane estate. Sir John was a brilliant senator, hardworking, witty, pugnacious. In the dying days of the Oireachtas that was then sitting he had tabled an amendment to the Creameries Acquisitions Bill that would have forced dairy disposal boards to publish audited accounts. On 20 May he had been forced to withdraw the same amendment. He also had to apologise for saying that if the general public knew all the facts about licensing and quotas the government would be blown sky-high. A week later he bounced back, asking if candidates seeking election would be free to express their views on neutrality.

"Any news of your son, Sir John?" the Deputy asked.

"None. But the news from Africa in general is good. The Germans will soon be driven out."

"I suppose neutrality will come up again in the election."

"Of course it will! The perception abroad is that Ireland is having a free ride."

"Couldn't possibly agree with that," replied the Deputy. "We've been very badly affected. What about the difficulties farmers are having, the inflation of prices? Indeed, Irishmen have lost their lives. You know yourself the figure for money-orders cashed at post offices last Christmas; fifty thousand money-orders. Each one of those represents an Irishman or woman working in England, part of the British war effort. And what about our ships being sunk on their way back home? No," mused the Deputy," we're not getting a free ride at all."

"The fighting, I mean. All the fighting is being done by the Allies. Perfidious Albion come to the rescue once again. If the Nazis win they'll hardly respect the niceties of Irish neutrality."

"There are sound historical reasons for our neutrality. The Six Counties question is the reality we have to live with down here."

Sir John looked at him and sighed. "Nothing changes, does it? Countries much bigger than the Free State have disappeared. Whole nations have been swallowed up by the Nazi war-machine. Yet we become more isolated with every day that passes."

The Deputy wondered what to say. How could he impress this extraordinary man? How strange that they both lived in the same small town, subject to the same civil authority, yet were miles apart politically. They were both Irishmen. But there was certainly more than one version of Irishness. The baronet represented his constituency faithfully, the constituency of business and agriculture. Like the Deputy, he had an acute and rooted sense of place, a deep belonging to Waterford and knowledge of its history. Sir John's family had lived on their patch of earth for at least four centuries.

"Don't you believe in the rights of property?" the Deputy piped up.

"Of course I do."

"Well then, you must apply your notion of property to the idea of neutrality. Neutrality is primarily a will to survive intact, in the face of forces that threaten to scatter one's inheritance."

"Ah, but one has obligations to other men of property. One has obligations to the community. Think of the experience that Ulster is having right now. Such a maturing experience, along with the rest of the world. It is so good for Ulster."

"I do think of that. But political interests will always reassert themselves in the end."

There was no give between them on the question. It was all bound up with the different interests and experiences that had shaped their characters.

By the time they reached Cappoquin station it was late evening. This time the platform was bustling: locals waiting for the delivery of the Dublin evening papers, wagons laden with rabbits and iced salmon, garagemen waiting for spare parts.

Sir John climbed down and waved in acknowledgement as one of his labourers came forward to take his bags. He turned to say goodbye to the Deputy," Well, another campaign ahead of you, Paudie."

"No rest for the wicked, sir!" the Deputy laughed. He saw Chrissie and Alice, who were standing near the white railing of the platform. "How are my beauties!" he shouted. They looked lovely in the evening sunshine. Alice was particularly stunning in a wine-coloured dress with an intricately crocheted white collar.

"Dada, you look tired," Chrissie greeted him.

"Dada is tired!" He kissed them both and handed his document case to Chrissie.

"There's no excitement about the election. Nobody seems to want it. Even Mr Lincoln is grumbling."

"Child, I'm fed up with the thing myself, and the only person I've canvassed so far is Sir John," the Deputy laughed. "Any word from your father, Alice?"

"Yes! He's in London now."

"Anything about business? He didn't say anything about the metal trade?"

"Of course he didn't," Chrissie chided her father.

"I'll show you his letter," Alice said. "He thinks I should consider joining him in England. There is so much work to be done. And I can type."

"But what about your safety. Is London safe?"

"There's so much great work to be done now. Staying safe doesn't really enter into it any more."

Chrissie nudged Alice. "Anyway, I persuaded her not to go. For God's sake what does she want to get herself killed for? There are air-raids every day."

"Not every day."

"You're staying here!" Chrissie pinched her arm. "Bobby would miss you so much."

"Bobby must mind himself," the Deputy said.

They walked together down the gravel avenue of the station. The early rhododendrons had begun to fade but the violently red hybrids were in full bloom. As they passed a lilac bush the Deputy snapped off a heavy bough. "For your mother," he said. Chrissie told him that Bobby had gone back to work in the forges. His arm was healed. Ellie'd had a relapse, though. She was terrified that she'd have to go to hospital, and convinced that she'd never return.

"Any word of your Lieutenant Kiely?"

The Deputy winked at Alice.

"Ah, that's Thursday's story," Alice said quickly, before Chrissie could say something.

"He called on Thursday," Chrissie explained.

"He gave her a present," Alice laughed.

"And why aren't you wearing it?" asked the Deputy.

"How could I wear it? It's a book."

"What's it called?"

"It's called *The Great O'Neill*. By Sean O'Faolain," said Alice.

"I couldn't get beyond page three," admitted Chrissie. "It's all about the bloody past. Just like a schoolbook."

"Admit it," said Alice. "The three pages you've read include the dedication and the contents."

"I don't know what you're talking about, girl."

"I must say he has lovely handwriting. Copperplate." Alice looked at Chrissie to make sure that she wasn't insulted.

"I see," said the Deputy," good handwriting. Rowing and handwriting and Cork Opera House. By God, this Kiely fellow is beginning to fill out a little."

CHAPTER ELEVEN

"I feel awful, Chrissie." Ellie rose awkwardly in the bed. Her left arm was stiff. The left side of her face was reddened by the starchy pillow. She looked terrible. "If I stay here much longer, I'll never rise again."

"You old fool. You will, of course." Chrissie spoke impatiently, playing at being completely adult. "You have one more month in bed. That's what the doctor said the last day. The summer is here. You'll soon be up and about."

But Ellie wouldn't be consoled. She had spent the idle morning tossing herself into a knot of sorrow. She repeated the phrase "never rise again" over and over. What broke her heart, she admitted, was that she would never be a bride. She wanted so much to be Mrs Kavanagh but now she had been robbed of that hope. "I may as well die now, rather than face a lonely life. What good am I to any man? I'm so sick...I've even affected your life, Chrissie. You've been taken out of school because of me. I know you hate housework."

"Listen, girl. I hate housework, but I hate bookwork even more."

"Chrissie, I'll never marry." Tears streamed down Ellie's face.

"God is good," Chrissie said. She ran to Ellie's bed and the two women hugged each other tearfully. While they were consoling each other, Bobby walked into the room, leaving in his wake a rush of laughter on the stairs. He had been working in the forges. There was a streak of black grease on his chin.

"Bobby!" Chrissie wiped her eyes with the pink sleeve of her cardigan. "Dry yourself," she said to Ellie.

"What's going on?" Bobby enquired.

"We were going over old times," said Chrissie.

"Forget about old times. Look who I've brought to see Ellie. Come in!" he shouted at the open doorway. In came Michael Kavanagh, hesitant and small like a newborn foal.

"Michael! My God!" Ellie exclaimed. "Did you tell Mrs Glenville that you were coming up here?"

"He came to see you, not my mother," Bobby laughed. "You'd like a cup of tea, Michael? And Ellie?"

Chrissie got the message. "Oh, right. I'll fix it. Mind you, it might be cocoa. I don't know what the tea situation is like."

"Oh Michael, you should have asked Mrs Glenville before coming upstairs." Ellie's first words were always of criticism: her lack of confidence ensured that if she couldn't think of what to say she would say something critical. She hadn't seen her fiancé for months. With the reticence of the rural poor he had barred himself from her bedside. He had come to the Glenvilles' front door several times to enquire after her health, but that was all. It took great courage on his part even to knock on that door, the door of a government deputy.

"You'll bloody well come upstairs with me, that's what I told him," said Bobby. "He was mooching at the door. You'll come and see your future wife. Isn't that what I said, Michael?"

"Did you clean your boots?" Ellie asked, this time less hostile.

Michael looked around nervously. He carried a small brown package.

Bobby winked at her. "Ah, Ellie, he was growing desperate to see you."

Ellie held out her hand. "Michael, it's great to see you. Your hair is long. You're very good."

"Kiss him, for the love of God," Bobby said.

"I made this for you," Michael said quietly, as if to rescue the situation. "You can put it on your bedside table." Ellie unwrapped the stiff brown paper wrapper, the kind of paper used in sugar bags. His gift was the result of a month's carving. It was a donkey, a donkey resting, carved from oak. It had been polished and buffed into a bright glaze. She rubbed the donkey's nose and then its back to see if the polish came off. It didn't.

"You're so gifted with your hands," Ellie said. "I must kiss you now."

He leaned forward and they kissed, without passion. "That hurts," she whispered, and he moved away because the donkey was pressing against her breasts. "It's staying there on the table where I can see it," she said.

"It's holy wood," he explained. "It came from an oak

that used to grow out of St Brigid's well near Sir John Keane's house. So it's a holy donkey. It will watch over you until I can watch over you."

"Bobby, do I hear Chrissie on the stairs?" Ellie gave the hint for him to push off.

"I'll have a look."

"It's such a peaceful donkey," she said. She took her fiancé's hand and kissed it. And when Bobby was out of earshot she whispered," I love you, Michael."

"It's been so lonely without you. I never had the guts to come up here before. I shouldn't have stayed away."

"It doesn't matter now. You're here." She pressed his hand to her face. He was about to say something when Chrissie and Bobby came back into the room.

"I hope you had a good chat," Chrissie said. "Here's some cocoa." There was an embarrassed silence before Ellie said thanks. "Mama's delighted that you came upstairs. She says to hell with gossipers. She says you must come more often now."

"What about gossipers?" Ellie asked, alarmed.

"Never mind that, for God's sake, Chrissie," Bobby snapped.

Ellie and Michael took their cups of cocoa. The other two found places to sit and remained in silence. The woodcarver looked at his donkey. Near his element, which was wood, he felt a greater strength. Beyond the nesting donkey, from the open window that looked out on to the street, came the sounds of a fair day. Cattle grunting, hooves clipping against the hard pavements, the barking of sheepdogs, men shouting, the honking of a rare motor-car or steam-truck: the open window filtered all these sounds that became a backdrop to the carved animal. "Cappoquin Fair," Chrissie said. "Dada has a big meeting today."

⁂

The Deputy knocked at the door of Mick L Ryall, the local newspaper reporter, who lived in Mass Lane. Mick was a correspondent for four provincial papers so his pen carried weight, but he had developed a style of journalism that would become commonplace in the following decades. He stayed at home, mostly in bed, and waited for the newsworthy to come clamouring to his door. It was an economic method of newsgathering. Some weeks nobody turned up with news, so Mick fell back on his store of old books, magazines, almanacs and local histories. Mick had one son, Patrick Declan, the apple of his eye, who played the piano every night, all night, in his bedroom. The insomniac musician was another reason for Mick's bed-based reporting.

"Go away!" Mick was shouting from his bedroom at the back of the cottage.

"Ah, come on, Mick! It's an important day. Big meetings! Don't miss our meeting, please don't. It's at four. Don't miss it!" The Deputy stooped to shout through the letter-box. It was like sending bottled messages down a river. Response not guaranteed. He felt movement on the pavement beside him. It was one of Brunnock's bullocks, escaped from Pound Lane. It had followed the Deputy from Cook Street. It nosed the barren flowerbox on Mick's window.

"I'm too tired. Patrick Declan had a bad night." Mick's voice crawled around the corner of the hall to the door.

"It's your duty! It's your duty as a journalist to be there!" The Deputy almost spat through the letterbox. That was too much for Mick. He leaped out of bed and stomped out of his bedroom. He stood at the end of his hallway. The Deputy could see his hairy legs and the yellowed end of a nightshirt.

"That's rich coming from you, Deputy Glenville! My duty! What's my duty? Go tell that to Dev and his bunch of censors. I'm not allowed to publish what I know. What about the harassment of IRA families and the corruption over vouchers. Isn't it my duty to report that! Go to hell, yourself and your party!"

"Don't let your country down, Mick," the Deputy replied quietly.

"FDR is the only politician worth writing about," said Mick. "When I was in America...Now, there's a country, there's a country. I remember the soup kitchens on the East Side. I remember the poverty of the immigrants. Immigrants shoved out of their homeland by you lot. God bless FDR. Have you ever seen a line of failed Irishmen, failed Italians, failed blacks. Well, I have. I've stood with them while I thought about home. If I hadn't hurt my hand I'd never have come back to this godforsaken country. Patrick Declan could be earning great money in America. He could have Carnegie Hall."

"Don't forget us, Mick. That piano of Patrick Declan's will need tuning some day. I'll get a tuner from Cork for you."

"You'd do that for my son?"

"I'd try, Mick."

"You might see me so."

"Don't forget us," the Deputy repeated. When he moved away from the house the bullock followed him. It trotted a few paces behind like a pony, as he walked up Main Street to call on Henchy's Medical Hall. Tim Henchy was the chairman of the local Fine Gael party. He would be presiding over the local Farmers' Party and Fine Gael meeting in the early afternoon. The Deputy needed something for an upset stomach. His stomach had been giving him trouble since April. Too much bad food, too much travelling.

"Maclean's Stomach Powder, that's what you should have," Mr Henchy said.

"Well done."

"One and sixpence."

The Deputy handed him a half-crown.

"Are ye expecting to lose? Is that what has the stomach rumbling?" Mr Henchy asked jovially.

"The election is as good as won," the Deputy replied loudly, for the benefit of the other customers in the pharmacy.

"Now, now, I don't believe that. The atmosphere has changed. You've been throwing out a lot of nasty stuff. Dev is in a panic."

"What nasty stuff?"

"Such as all the talk about neutrality, such as questioning our own stand on the Emergency."

"You are a bit weak on neutrality."

"Nonsense, man." Mr Henchy handed the Deputy a shilling change. "Neutrality was in the constitution of 1922. Our right to be neutral was always maintained by my party, at parliamentary conferences, at the League of Nations and at imperial conferences. As far back as 1925..."

The Deputy stopped him in his tracks. "A change of government would be dangerous in these times."

"Not half as dangerous as incompetence."

"We all do our best," the Deputy said, trying to be smart. He looked at the two customers for support, but none was forthcoming. "We all do our best in these times," he repeated. "Well, I must be off. There's a busy day ahead." He left the shop and walked towards the busy town square. The bullock was still following him. But when he reached the square the animal turned left up Pound Lane. The Deputy was relieved. But he was troubled by the confidence shown by Mr Henchy. And he had been so lucid, so well-briefed. The opposition men must have been given advice by their headquarters.

≈

Later that day, when the business of the fair was over, the public meetings began. Fine Gael and the Farmers' Party candidates stood on the platform together; each candidate emphasised the value of agriculture and the heroism of the farmers who fed the country. "If it wasn't for the farmer, every man, woman and child in this country would starve!" declared one speaker. The crowd cheered wildly. It was a time of great self-satisfaction in the agricultural world.

When the opposition speakers had finished, the government candidates mounted the platform. There was a great deal of confusion in the streets as government supporters moved forward and farmers headed back to the pub or to tend their animals.

When all the farmers and opposition supporters had moved away, there was only a small crowd left. The Deputy and young Ned Kenny had hoped to do better than that. But Ned Lonergan and Tom Lincoln weren't surprised. "Transport problems," Tom Lincoln said to Paddy Little, who had motored all the way from Waterford City.

"A lot of people from Lismore said that they'd come. But I don't see them," said Senator Goulding.

The Deputy scanned the crowd for the tall figure of Mick L Ryall, but Mick was nowhere to be seen. Bobby climbed on to the platform. "Well done," his father said. "You're good to come along." With his son beside him the Deputy felt stronger.

"You can start, Tom," Senator Goulding said to Mr Lincoln. Tom Lincoln moved to the front of the platform and began to address the crowd. Mr Little then spoke for five minutes, and after him Senator Goulding, who was well known in the locality. Finally, the Deputy said a few words. He praised the crowd and the locality for their loyalty in the past. He praised the Party for its leadership during the Emergency. Dev, he went on, was like a father to the whole nation; he was like a great big Tom Lincoln. That made the crowd laugh. He said that the shortages being experienced were nothing compared to the suffering of people in Europe. "We are blessed with a fertile country," the Deputy continued, "and we are standing here now in the middle of one of the most beautiful and fertile areas in the world. We shouldn't worry about our isolation. With Dev at the helm we can withstand all danger."

"What about the imprisonment of Republicans?" A voice suddenly rose from the sheepish crowd. There was an expectant silence.

The Deputy rounded on the questioner. "Only those who constitute a threat are behind bars. There are ample proofs of contact between illegal organisations and a belligerent power. Only the other day, if any of you are in the habit of listening to Hitler's programmes on the wireless, you would have heard that Ireland was criticised and Mr de Valera was criticised. Our enemies must know that Dev will give us tough government."

The questioner appeared to be satisfied; there were no further questions. It was quite possible that he didn't want to give away his location in the crowd to the two guards on duty. The Deputy thanked the crowd for their attention and thanked the man for his question. He was winding down the address when another voice shouted, "Let Bobby give us a song!"

The Deputy laughed. "Bobby isn't a candidate!"

"Give us a song, Bobby," a tall aristocratic-looking man demanded. It was Paddy Dineen, a well-known process-server. He dressed like a tramp and he lived in one of the labourers' cottages owned by the local convent. The nuns had been trying to evict him for years but he was too crafty. They had never succeeded in serving him with an eviction order.

"Give us a song!" another voice demanded. The crowd became animated. There was no way out of it. They had discovered something more interesting than policies.

"Go on, so," the Deputy said to his son. He winked at Mr Little, who seemed to be worried. The minister relaxed.

"What'll I sing?" Bobby asked.

They wanted something from Wallace. The love of light opera extended throughout Co Waterford.

"Rose Marie!" a female voice shouted. Bobby replied that it would have to be something from *Maritana*.

"All right so," the female voice was gracious.

Bobby cleared his throat and found his key. He sang "In Happy Moments Day by Day" with terrific grace and sweetness. The little bell of the Protestant church struck four as he sang; the bell-sound filling the warm air gave authority to his words, somehow, and lent a dreamlike atmosphere to the passing minutes. In the June afternoon, with the rest of the world at war, all were happy to be a part of the song. A young man singing at the height of his power on a fair day reminded the audience that their own children didn't have to go to war. This was the happy moment that the Party promised.

While his son was singing, the Deputy noticed a face in the crowd. It was the Old IRA Commandant from Dungarvan, come to question him, no doubt, about the fate of the young IRA man. "Blast it," whispered the Deputy in Tom Lincoln's ear. "I knew it couldn't last."

"The old comrade, is it?"

"Yes."

"Tell him you've done your best. That's the truth, isn't

it? There's a limit to what can be done."

When Bobby finished his song, the crowd applauded and called for more. But the Deputy moved forward and reminded them that it was long after four. There were people from the Melleray district who had a long way to go. "There are womenfolk here, too," he joked, "whose men will be screaming for their suppers!" That put an end to the demands.

"There were a hundred first preferences in that song," Bobby said to his father.

"You're worth more than that, son." The Deputy tapped him affectionately on the shoulder.

෴

"Is there a drop left in that pot?" asked the captain. He was a notorious tea-drinker. The other officers, including Lieutenant Kiely, had given up the hope of further refreshments. They had had a bad night of manoeuvres. At midnight, word had come through that an "illegal organisation" (which could mean only the IRA) might land a supply of guns in Youghal harbour and transfer them up-river on the tide. The officers and their men had spent a wet night at the mouth of the Blackwater. Their only encounter had indeed been a hostile one, but it wasn't related to political subversion. In the pitch darkness they had intercepted a small fishing-boat, where they found a naked and irate Labour Party county councillor and a shivering, nearly naked woman. The woman was the daughter of a local Protestant landowner whose property had been commandeered by the army. All the officers volunteered to see the woman home: the councillor insisted on making his own way. "What a night," the captain said again," what a bloody laugh."

"I wonder if someone was out to get the Labour man?" remarked an older officer from Co Meath.

"It crossed my mind." The captain poured what remained in the teapot into his cup. "Some jealous bastard. You can imagine the local jealousy over a good-looking ascendancy woman."

"It's such a phoney war," the Co Meath officer said. He marked the page and closed his book, William Bulfin's *Rambles in Eireann*. He had been reading silently through their late breakfast. "Christ, but there's a cold wind up here." They were having breakfast outdoors, in the courtyard of the Big House that was their HQ. The captain's continental memories, the camping holidays in Austria, the walks through Germany, made him insist on outdoor eating. The others were fed up with cold food.

"Are you enjoying the book?" asked the captain.

"Wonderful," the older officer replied. "*There's* a man who loved Ireland. He's just after encountering a Jewish peddler and he says that the whole lot of the Jews should be run out of the country."

"He was a Hitlerite, so," the lieutenant commented.

"At least Hitler has tried to solve the Jewish problem."

"What Jewish problem? What problem?" the lieutenant asked, annoyed.

"Take it easy," the captain interjected, but the other officer continued.

"You know damn well yourself. Usury, the control that they have over world finance. They controlled everything that moved in Europe before Hitler put his foot down."

"Don't be ridiculous. They've been the most persecuted people in history. We think we've had a rotten time from the English; by Christ it's nothing to what the Jews have suffered. Everybody has a go at the Jews."

"Herr Hitler is solving the problem."

"There's no problem," the lieutenant replied harshly. "The problem is with us, with us Catholics. It's our anti-Jewish attitude. We've been brought up to despise the Jews."

"They crucified Christ!"

"Since when were you so worried about Christ? You don't even go to Mass when you're on leave. Remember Jesus was a Jew, he came from a good Jewish family. The House of David and all that."

"Christ, since when did you become such a Jew-lover?" The officer from Co Meath rose from his chair and claimed his jacket. He stalked away.

The others laughed. "Take no notice of him," the captain said. "He's just pissed off that you got the job to bring the half-naked woman home. Did she try anything? You're a handsome lad."

"Divil a bit," the lieutenant lied.

CHAPTER TWELVE

All the national newspapers reported great enthusiasm for Mr Cosgrave and his colleagues. The government responded by putting more canvassers on the ground and by trying to undermine public confidence in Fine Gael's will to remain neutral. Dev himself worked harder and harder: in one weekend of torrential rain he addressed eight public meetings in Co Clare, speaking for at least an hour on each occasion. He was indefatigable. Government spokesmen echoed the Taoiseach's words. Mr MacEntee, speaking in Dublin, said that the one serious issue facing the country was the security of the state. Other speakers scoffed at the idea of a "national government," saying that it was first and foremost an "*Irish Times* kite" that had been blown up into a balloon by Fine Gael and was now burst into smithereens. The mixed metaphors created few laughs at public meetings.

Accompanied by the Deputy and Senator Goulding, Mr Little spoke to his home-crowd in Ferrybank near Waterford, in early June. Again he tried to show that the inexperience of the opposition was a danger to the country. "Not all parties or party leaders have behind them the experience of facing belligerents at close quarters." He claimed that it was the Republican movement that saved Ireland from conscription in 1917 and 1918, and that Fianna Fáil was the direct heir to that tradition.

It seemed as if nothing could stem the flow of sympathy away from the government. The majority of the newspapers championed the Fine Gael leadership. All papers reported the enthusiasm with which Mr Cosgrave was greeted—even in Co Clare, the Taoiseach's own constituency. When he spoke in south Kerry, Dev referred to the bias of the newspapers: "They are as bitter against us today as they ever were. Those who have been reading them have their minds poisoned against Fianna Fáil." But the newspapers were suffering only from a common enough complaint, a combination of boredom and anger over censorship. This boredom filtered through even to Mick L Ryall, who ignored the election in his weekly columns and wrote instead on the dangers of roaming bullocks and straying donkeys. When the Deputy tackled him on the street one day Mick replied that he had spent the afternoon of the meetings in bed, but that he was sorry to have missed Bobby's lyrical contribution to the great debates of the day.

After Fine Gael held a triumphal public meeting in Waterford on the third Thursday of June, the local Party stepped up its canvassing. Mr Cosgrave's entry into Waterford had been a triumph: he was granted the freedom of the city, and thousands shouted themselves hoarse with enthusiasm. The Deputy, along with Tom Lincoln and Ned Kenny, planned a series of canvassing trips that would maximise the use of the eight-gallon petrol ration available to each candidate. The Deputy would make circular drives through the countryside, stopping at designated cross-roads and villages. In that way the Deputy met an enormous number of Party faithful in those middle weeks of June. Party followers would gather around a few banners and posters. Party officials sent their wives and children into the fields to work so that the opposition couldn't say that they were contributing to the labour shortage. Night had often fallen by the time the Deputy reached his final meeting point. Once, near Ballymacarbery, a village in the hills, a resourceful Party group rigged up a public lighting system using a carbide generator. The locals were so delighted with the device that people stayed around for the whole night, chatting and laughing.

The daylight hours, the long pungent days of new June growth, left their mark on the Party canvassers. Some young men who joined the Party at this time were excited and enchanted beyond measure by the early summer wartime political journey. So was Ned Kenny. The joy was as much in the canvass as the thought of winning. For many in the deep countryside, the summer of 1943 seemed like an enchanted time. Life stood still.

But it was in the village of Modeligo, Ned's home-place, that he received his true baptism as a Party man. "You introduce me!" the Deputy said to him, when a crowd of about forty had gathered.

"Jasus, I couldn't. What can I say? What do I know?"

"You know these people," said Tom Lincoln. "That's more important than anything else."

And Ned, crushing a bundle of handbills in his fist, walked up to the platform (three planks thrown across the corner of a garden wall) and addressed the crowd. He trembled. But the crowd, recognising their native son, cheered him. Ned spoke ten words in all, not in any coherent order," The Deputy...welcome...I just want to say...Party...Glenville." The crowd cheered again. Afterwards, because he had spoken from the platform, people approached him and shook his hand.

"This is Mrs Hallie," the Deputy said.

"Hello, Ma'am."

"You will be a great speaker. A man of the future."

"Are you Mick Kenny's son?"

"A cousin."

"You have the public man in you, so. Mick was a champion dancer."

"Thanks."

Two days later, they thought the canvass would be so relaxed that they brought Chrissie and Alice with them, but they ran into a pocket of *Aiséirí* supporters, anarchist Republicans, who tried to smash their placards and board-mounted posters. The *Aiséirí* men were protesting at the conditions of imprisonment of IRA prisoners. The meeting was held eight miles from the nearest guards barracks, so the Party followers had to weather the abuse. Chrissie was the least tolerant. When she saw an *Aiséirí* man daubing posters with cow shit, she ran across the street and slapped him violently across the face. The dauber retreated. And the crowd, seeing the man's humiliation, burst into laughter.

"And what about the poor, the unemployed?" another

protester shouted.

"We've spent over a million pounds on unemployment assistance, and we introduced the Widows and Orphans Pensions Act," the Deputy replied.

"You lock people up. Coercion!" shouted another.

"The country must be protected from enemies within."

*

The day after that encounter with the *Aiséirí* men the Deputy received a second letter about the condemned IRA man. This time it was from Dev's office: an offer of a meeting with the Taoiseach on Thursday, 1 July, the day of the opening of the new Dáil. The Deputy was delighted. He felt he had really broken through. He brought the letter into the kitchen to show it to Adele. "About the IRA lad," he said," I think something is going to be done."

"Dada, your face is bleeding," said Chrissie.

The Deputy rubbed his hands over his cheeks and looked at the spots of blood that came away. "So it is. I must change from those 7-o'clock slotted blades. They don't suit me."

"You'll be meeting Dev. That's wonderful. Wonderful." Adele was as excited as himself. "Maybe they won't hang the poor boy at all."

"Would Fine Gael hang Dev if the government was defeated?" asked Emer.

Adele laughed. "They would if they thought they'd get away with it."

The Deputy read the Taoiseach's letter again. "This could

be the beginning..."

"You have done well," Adele said proudly.

But the Deputy repeated that it was only the beginning. Dev was a tough man, he had to be tough in these desperate times. "Let's hope my first preference vote goes up. Then I can face him with more confidence."

"Can I go canvassing with you tomorrow?" asked Chrissie.

"Depends on Captain Mulvey. Whether he'll let us all on the boat."

"He'll do what you say."

"Right. You can come. But you must help us with the canvass."

"Alice should come too."

The Deputy raised no objection. Captain Mulvey had a big boat.

⋅⋅

On the following day, at high tide, the Deputy and five Party men as well as Chrissie, Alice and Bobby boarded Captain Mulvey's steamer. They were laden with Party literature, posters and small packages of sandwiches. The steamer would head southwards on the falling tide, and they would return in the evening when the tide turned. Ned Kenny estimated that the journey by steamer would save three gallons of petrol and the Party would have to pay only for the wood to keep the boiler operating.

"It's so beautiful," Alice said to Bobby as the boat steamed away, its blades cutting into the placid waters.

It was indeed another perfect wartime summer's day, with hardly a cloud in the sky. An early-morning shower had cleared the air so that everything on the river-bank glowed and stiffened in the sun.

"I should have put on some make-up," Chrissie said.

"Oh I don't think so," Alice replied. "The breeze is so good for one's face. All that fresh air."

"Are you going to *Charley's Aunt* with the Lieutenant?" asked Bobby.

"I am."

"Did you tell *him*?" Bobby enquired, pointing to his father. "Are you sure he'll let you go to Cork again?"

"It hasn't been mentioned," Chrissie said, in a tone that left no doubt about her desire to drop the subject. The girls waved at a group of men and children washing milk-churns in the river.

The Deputy and Ned shouted from the stern: "Don't forget Goulding and Glenville. Glenville and Goulding. Be sure and vote!" The churn-cleaners waved back and booed. Swear-words drifted across the river.

"Definitely not Party faithful," Captain Mulvey observed. "Camphire in five minutes."

When they reached the district of Camphire the Party men left the boat and headed off in the direction of a cluster of houses. Captain Mulvey and Bobby stayed behind to load a supply of logs on board. "We'll be over an hour here. You should stretch your legs with the Deputy," the captain said to Chrissie and Alice. The two women disembarked and followed the Deputy, who in turn was following the Party men.

They returned an hour later, the canvassing done. The Deputy carried two long white gutted rabbits. "Mrs Whelan gave me these. She said they're great for a stew." He had no intention of eating them. The idea of eating rabbit made him want to vomit.

"You don't have to worry about the agricultural labourers and river poachers," one of the Party men advised the Deputy. "And avoid Hennessys' house in this area."

"Why's that?"

"The Hennessys are still upset over the Economic War. Last time we called the missus went into a tantrum over what Dev did to her family. They used to have a big export trade to England. The Economic War destroyed all that."

"I'm sorry for them," the Deputy said. "I remember that name, and the liquidation sale. The Party made a lot of enemies in business then."

"Their daughters go with soldiers now. Loose, you know. Soldiers, not officers, I mean," the man said quickly. It had just occurred to him that the Deputy's daughter was seeing an army man.

By lunchtime they had steamed to within three miles of Youghal, the Deputy's home-place. The captain manoeuvred the craft into the deep central channel of the river-mouth. They made tea while waiting for the tide to fill. While they ate their sandwiches they stared at the broad expanse of water. At that point in the river, south of Strancally Castle, the water was broad and placid, and the steep river-banks were covered with lush deciduous trees. They watched river birds diving from the tree-tops, skimming the water. Captain Mulvey's dog, Moll, barked at the birds that came too close.

After she had eaten, Chrissie felt a great need to go to the toilet, but there was no toilet on board. Captain Mulvey sensed her anxiety. He emerged from his perch astern, carrying a large bucket. "If anyone wishes to relieve themselves they can do so in this, in the wheelhouse." Bobby was delighted. But Chrissie would let her bladder burst before submitting to the humiliation of a bucket.

By the time the tide had turned, four of the men on board had used the bucket. Then they began the journey homewards. On that journey they concentrated on the clusters of population on the eastern bank of the river. By the time they reached the slipway at Villierstown it was four in the afternoon. The Deputy and the Party workers disembarked. Chrissie followed them enthusiastically. She turned around to wait for Alice, but Alice remained in the boat with Bobby. The emphasis of relationships had altered in the boat. Bonding had occurred, and Chrissie understood. Momentarily, she envied Alice.

Bobby and Alice loitered on board, chatting with Captain Mulvey. The tide-filled river was particularly beautiful at this point: the broad water and the rich farmland of Tourin were fused together in the heat-haze of the afternoon. Fish rose in the deep pools and swallows dived in pursuit of insects. A pheasant's scratching voice could be heard in the distance. "That's a real summer sound, I always say," said the captain. But the two loiterers didn't reply. They wanted to be alone. Alice wanted to talk, Bobby to make love.

"Alice and I will go for a walk," Bobby said to Captain Mulvey.

"Do. Yes, of course," the captain agreed. "A walk will be good for you both. Why don't you stroll along the river-bank. But mind the hidden inlets."

The two clambered on to the slipway and began their walk. When they were out of Captain Mulvey's sight Bobby said, "Can I call you Asya now? I haven't called you by your right name since St Patrick's Day. Do you remember?" Alice took his hand and said that that day had never left her mind. This encouraged Bobby. He stopped in his tracks, pulling her to him. He kissed her hungrily, determined to hold her. Alice squirmed free.

"Please, Bobby, it's no use. Our beginning something deep. We can't go on teasing ourselves. I can't commit myself."

"We'll see. Do you not like the feeling of being kissed?"

"Of course I love it! I'm a woman. But kissing makes it even more difficult. It weakens me."

"That's what I want it to do!" Bobby laughed.

"We've hardly spoken in three months," complained Alice. "I have so much to tell you."

"What?"

"I may have to go away. I haven't heard from my father for weeks now. But in his last letter he hinted heavily that I should prepare to leave."

"Ireland is the safest place. The Germans won't invade Ireland. They like Ireland. You'd be safe here." Bobby touched her face, but she withdrew from him. "I *know*! Maybe I could go to England with you. I could help."

"You couldn't. My father wouldn't allow it. Your father wouldn't allow it. Anyway, it's religious work."

"But you told me you had no religion now."

"I mean war work, Bobby. To be honest, it's all war work."

"I'm going to lose you, Asya."

"Please call me Alice."

"But the name Asya gets to you, doesn't it? It touches a part of you, the deep part. You don't feel any loyalty to the name Alice. When I use it it doesn't touch you. But Asya, Asya, it touches your heart. It's you."

"Sometimes you can be so sensitive."

"Sometimes?"

"Yes."

"Thanks very much."

They walked on until they came to a stand of laurel bushes and lime trees that had been planted at the river-bank by the Villiers-Stuart family. They sat down at an enclosed patch of grass by the river. The scent of laurel and lauristinus was heavy in the air. "Please, Bobby, be responsible," Alice said suddenly as they touched the warm ground. Bobby drew her to himself and kissed her again. She responded. She allowed his hand to wander, from her skirt to her blouse. He touched her breasts and that excited her. "We must be careful," she said. "We must be." But Bobby had neither the maturity nor the experience to check himself or pace his pleasure. Alice was soon pinned to the ground by his heavy body, struggling but still more annoyed than frightened. "Be gentle, please!" When his hand lifted her skirt and tried to part her thighs she became more desperate. "Let me sit up! Bobby! Let me sit up; I can't breathe!"

"No. I want you to myself, for myself," he muttered. "You said there was this special bond between us. You said that twelve weeks ago."

"Don't," pleaded Alice. "Not this. Bobby! Bobby!" She could feel his will collapsing. His weight upon her lessened and she saw that he was crying.

"I'm sorry, Alice. I nearly raped you. I'm such an idiot. I knew you didn't want to. I thought I could make you want it."

"Yes, you can. You could. But not now. We have so much to talk about." She stretched out her hand to touch him but he pulled away violently. As violently as he had previously held her down. "Don't be upset, it's just a misunderstanding."

"Yes, that's it. That's my life. A misunderstanding." He cried. "I can't get through to anyone."

"You get through to me, Bobby. But I'm frightened. I don't know what's going on between us now. I never had a boyfriend before."

The words soothed him. He could identify with her innocence. They restored his ego. "I nearly raped you," he whispered.

"You didn't. Please get that notion out of your head." She began to brush her clothes. Her blouse was covered with dead grasses and seeds. She started to pluck them off.

Bobby stood up. He didn't offer to help. He was afraid to go near her now. "I'm going back to the boat."

Alice looked up at him and felt a great tenderness. It was the tenderness of the strong for the weak. What she knew about the world, about the rape of innocents, her own people, the European Jews; what she knew about suffering, would overwhelm him. "Please wait for me," she said firmly, knowing that he would wait.

The Deputy and the others were already on the boat when they climbed in. "You were supposed to help us," the Deputy said accusingly. "Where were you?" Then he looked at Alice and his anger diminished. He immediately saw her distress, the evidence of a struggle or a tumble, grass on her blouse. She hadn't done a good job of tidying up. "Alice, dear, are you all right?"

Alice looked at him mournfully. Then she began to cry.

"What's the meaning of this? Dear God, what did you do, boy? Answer me!" The Deputy's face was scarlet with fury.

His son stared ahead, at the pile of cut rhododendrons and laurels that Captain Mulvey had collected for the Corpus Christi Procession. He always decorated the bacon-factory gates with flowers and leaves. The bow was flower-bedecked, like a funeral ship. Bobby said nothing.

"Answer me, Bobby! What have you done?" the Deputy persisted. "Look at me when I speak to you!"

Bobby looked at him. "We had a bit of a scrape," he said casually. "Alice fell when we tried to get up the bank to look down on the river. It's nothing."

The Deputy looked at Alice. "Well, child?" he asked. "Was there trouble between you two?"

"I...I struggled," Alice said. "I fell. I got a terrible fright."

"We should have stayed with you, Dada," said Bobby. "We could have helped you."

"You certainly could," his father replied angrily.

CHAPTER THIRTEEN

Chrissie opened the *Cork Examiner* again and located the column headed "Military Weddings." Ever since she had become seriously interested in Lieutenant Kiely she had made a habit of reading about weddings. The whole subject had come into sharper focus. Now she read an account of the wedding of a commandant in the southern command. Ellie looked up at her from the nest of propped pillows. "Listen to this, will you. Listen. 'The bride wore a two-piece lagoon blue ensemble, with pink trimmings, and carried a shower bouquet of roses. Miss Moira Baker (sister) was bridesmaid, and the best man was Lieutenant OG Dowling, brother of the groom. The officers' guard of honour included Captains Little, Swanson, O'Sullivan, Lieutenants Buckler, Cullen, McCarthy and O'Brien.'"

Ellie was impressed. "So many men! Lieutenant Kiely must know those officers. Do you think he'll have a guard of honour when he marries?"

"Of course he will!...They're spending their honeymoon in the South of Ireland."

"Isn't that where we live?"

"It is. God help us, there isn't much fun in that. The bride's going-away outfit was a báinín tweed suit, with pink and navy accessories..."

"I wouldn't like pink with navy."

"Neither would I," Chrissie agreed. She put down the paper. Marriage was the great interest that she and Ellie shared. Across the page from the "Weddings" section was an energetic report of the Allied landings in Sicily.

"You're looking so well today, Ellie."

"I'm going to be up by the end of the month. Then I can pay back your mother all the money I owe her. I'm going to work round the clock."

"You will not. You'll take it easy." Chrissie picked up the paper again and scanned the front-page advertisements. "I wonder how Dada is doing in Dublin. There's terrible shortages in the cities."

It was a bad election for the Deputy and the Party. On polling day, the day after Corpus Christi, huge crowds had come into town to vote. The Party had organised dozens of ponies and traps, cabs and outside cars to transport the old and the isolated to the polling booths. The turnout of voters had been very high—in some districts over ninety per cent. While people gathered at the polling stations they discussed the shortages of food and petrol, and the war in the world outside. On the night of Corpus Christi there had been massive Anglo-American air-raids on continental Europe. Sixty-nine Allied planes had been lost. The Party faithful who came to vote were grateful for the absence of war, yet they marvelled at the sheer volume of manpower and materials involved in battle. The men, especially, wallowed in the extraordinary statistics of bomb-loads and Axis forces captured or killed.

The Party vote fell dramatically. The vote in Waterford fell from twenty-two thousand to eighteen, a huge drop. The Deputy's own vote fell by fifteen hundred. He held his seat, but was morally and politically weakened. He was nervous about his coming encounter with Dev. The election itself had been ill-timed, because of the food shortages which were at their worst in May and June.

Despite the drop of ten per cent in his party vote, De Valera succeeded in being re-elected Taoiseach when the eleventh Dáil met on 1 July. The Deputy was relieved that Dev was still in power. He checked with the Taoiseach's office to see if his meeting held good. It was on. The Taoiseach's secretary told him that he was expected on the following Saturday instead. He rang Adele to see if there had been any further communications from the family of the IRA man or from the old O/C but there was nothing.

"Did you meet Alice's father?" asked Adele. On the day that the eleventh Dáil met, Alice's father arrived in Ireland. He was visiting Dublin Jews about his war work. On his way to lunch with one of the Briscoe family he had met the Deputy to hear news of Alice, his Asya.

"For God's sake, don't say anything to Alice. She knows nothing about her father's visit. She'd be heartbroken if she knew he was so close and hadn't phoned or come to see her."

"Bobby is very well-behaved. Didn't he even get a lift to Youghal and clean your parents' grave. He says it was in a state."

"Good, good."

"He's making an effort, he really is," Adele said. She had succeeded in putting off what might have been a violent exchange between Bobby and his father over Bobby's attitude to Alice. Bobby had upset her, that was all the Deputy knew. But it was enough. As the Deputy learned more about the atrocities committed against Jews (and Alice's father had a store of new tales of Nazi barbarism) his sense of responsibility towards Alice intensified.

"He has been very good lately," Adele repeated, mending bridges.

"That's a relief."

&

The following Saturday the Deputy walked from his flat to his meeting with the Taoiseach. He needed the long walk to prepare himself. He repeated Sean T O'Kelly's words over and over in his mind: "We are the lineal descendants of Sinn Féin and we've taken the torch from them to carry on the fight for freedom." The words became like a prayer before battle. He intended to quote the words at the Taoiseach, who was an old soldier of the Republic.

He had to wait twenty minutes. In the ante-room there was a statue of Lincoln and a copy of the American Declaration of Independence. Although high-windowed, the room had resisted the penetration of July sunlight, so it was cold. The Deputy surveyed the thick carpet and was startled from his secret recital of O'Kelly's words by the loud noise of a clock striking the quarter-hour. Eventually he was ushered inside. Dev was still speaking on the telephone in Irish. When he stopped the Deputy began:

"*Dia is Muire dhuit. Táim an-bhuíoch díot as bheith anseo.. Is cuimhin liom an t-am a bhí mé féin...*"

"*Ná h-abair é.*" Dev waved his left hand. "You've come to me about the condemned man."

The Deputy was relieved to hear the English words, though he had been prepared to argue through Irish. "He's hardly a man, only a boy."

"Man enough to use a gun. You told my secretary that this man intends to intensify his hunger-strike. I've gone hungry myself, I don't remember any grades of hunger."

"His mother says that he's going to stop taking water," the Deputy said earnestly. He hated to begin with the hunger-strike angle. Dev detested moral blackmail because he had used it so often himself. IRA men had already been shot by firing-squad. He had proved his ability to ride Republican anger.

"You realise, Deputy, that these men would usurp the authority of the state. We can't bend in the face of threat." The Taoiseach moved forward in his chair and stared at the Deputy with his incredibly cold eyes. His face was fatter than usual and his skin was pale rather than sallow. The lack of fresh air, the Deputy thought. An excess of closed rooms. The war had imprisoned him behind state doors, behind steel-rimmed glasses. His hair was soft and brown. He looked round. "Do you understand what we're up against? If we allow one sign of weakness, one crack, one little crack in our resolve, Mr Churchill or Herr Hitler will be down on top of us with savage demands. You have to be tough to be neutral. There are no shoulders to cry on. Right now, Deputy, our country has no friends, *no* friends!"

"He was only a boy when he shot that policeman. What does he know? His head was full of patriotism."

"He shot a detective-sergeant. He was part of the larger conspiracy to get this country involved in a war. Last year we had Mr Dillon and his Allied friends. Now we have the IRA and their German parachutists. The detective was a father of four children. He was a cousin of the Minister for Supplies."

"I knew the boy's father. Johnny. He fought with the West Waterford Brigade. Refused a pension. The boy was born destitute and the family lives in destitution still. They are very idealistic people."

"Nevertheless, he committed a capital offence."

"We did worse when we fought the British."

"We were fighting a just war. We were the army of the Dáil, just as Lincoln's army was the army of congress."

"But not in 1916. In 1916 there was no Dáil. When Seán T addressed our convention in Dungarvan he talked about the Party's Republican pedigree. He said that we were the lineal descendants of Sinn Féin. A lot of Republicans just see England's difficulty. A chance to strike."

"My dear Deputy." Dev took a deep breath, a breath of exasperation. "The state is the descendant of Sinn Féin. This state and its sovereign government elected by the majority of the Irish people are the legitimate descendants of Sinn Féin. Anyone who attacks this state or its servants is an enemy of the Irish majority, the historical majority that's been there since the time of O'Connell."

The black box of the telephone rang again. The whole room vibrated. Dev lifted the receiver from its black claws and listened. *"Tá go maith,"* he said. *"Amárach, ar a h-aon déag. Tá go maith."* He put down the phone.

"We are threatened on all sides, Deputy. There are conspirators everywhere. Did you not feel threatened at any time during the election campaign. I can't believe you didn't. Dr Ryan had to be protected from a mob in Limerick and Dan Breen was abused in Emly. Party literature was destroyed and leaflets threatening our members were handed out after Mass. I myself was heckled by an hysterical woman in Enniscorthy. In south Kerry I had to listen to wild men screaming 'Coercion.' We cannot allow the country to slip into anarchy."

He leaned forward and looked at the Deputy intensely, like an examining optician. "We have to be firm against the internal threats. In that way we send signals to outsiders. Do you understand?"

"I do, *a Thaoisigh*. But I'm thinking of my poor constituents. The boy's family, his poor mother." Hope was receding. He placed both hands on the Taoiseach's desk. "Surely there is a place for compassion. Twenty years ago a lot of our best people were the victims of summary execution. We thought we'd seen an end.to executions."

"This has not been, will not be, a summary execution. I resent your use of those words. The evidence has been heard and judgement handed down. This is the law."

"But compassion, there must be room for compassion," the Deputy pleaded.

"Compassion! What compassion did the IRA show for

the detective? The man was the father of four children. It is a terrible thing to be fatherless."

"The family will go crazy with grief. It will make the Republicans even more bitter against us."

"I am sorry. God knows, I am sorry. Hanging is a terrible way to die."

"Can nothing be done?"

"Nothing." The Taoiseach glanced restlessly at his papers. There was a file on the condemned man that he hadn't even opened. The Deputy knew that his time was up. "By the way, I see that your own vote has fallen dramatically."

"We all suffered, Taoiseach. It's a miracle that we hung on to power, with a ten per cent loss over the whole country."

"One more reason why we must stand firm against the enemies of the state. If illegal elements get in touch with you, I'd like you to pass on my firmness of purpose. You would be doing a valuable service to your country and to your constituents."

He was dismissed. The Taoiseach stood up and shook his hand firmly. "I'm sorry. Our neutral position has created much suffering. But those sufferings are nothing compared to the infinite destruction of all-out war."

The Deputy didn't thank the Taoiseach. He had achieved absolutely nothing. A cold spasm of shock rose through his body as he walked the Dublin streets. The heat of July had no effect. He was to blame. He had been ill-prepared for such an important meeting. He should have pleaded only on compassionate grounds. He had made a mistake in somehow trying to mitigate the crime. The Taoiseach had been provoked into a defence of the party position, a rationalisation of Mr O'Kelly's convention speech. The physical safety of the people, citizens of the state, was what was paramount. He had made a great mistake in playing the Sinn Féin card.

When he reached the flat he telephoned home to give Adele the bad news. "There's no give, no hope," he said, dejected.

"You mustn't give up that easily," she insisted. "Keep writing letters. Write to the papers, write to the Minister for Justice."

"What can I say to the poor man's family? Surely nobody deserves to die. Not in this day and age."

"You mustn't fall apart. The main thing is to keep pressing. It's not all defeat."

"Don't tell me there's some good news?"

"You won't believe it. Mrs Hallissey got off." Mrs Hallissey had been prosecuted by the Minister for Supplies for defying the Control of Prices Order nearly eighteen months previously. She had sold a quarter-pound of tea for one shilling while the controlled price was three shillings and fourpence per pound, and she had sold a tin of Fry's cocoa for ninepence while the controlled price was sixpence. The Deputy knew that she had another charge pending for selling a pot of apple and strawberry jam for double the controlled price. The judge dismissed her case because the overcharging incidents had been reported more than three months after they had occurred. But nothing would prevent Mrs Hallissey from believing that it was the Deputy's influence. "So it's not all bad news," Adele said cheerfully.

"There was a life at stake here," the Deputy reminded her.

"I know, my love." She was not going to be depressed. She knew he was in trouble. "You mustn't allow this to ruin your other work. So many people need you."

"Did the Kellehers get my telegram?" Dillie Kelleher, the daughter of the local station-master, and a friend of Chrissie's had been married that day to a Lieutenant Dooley from Dublin. Adele had spent the previous day helping Dillie's mother with the baking for the wedding breakfast, which was held in the station house.

"They did. Dillie was thrilled. She looked so beautiful. I'm not long back from the house. Chrissie was eying her lieutenant. She had him in her grip. The poor boy couldn't escape."

"Chrissie's too young."

"They're marrying younger and younger nowadays."

"Will you stop matchmaking!" the Deputy said, his humour getting better. "Is Chrissie there now? I'd like to have a few words with her." Adele called to Chrissie, who was in the living-room listening to the gramophone. Bobby had bought a new record of Geraldo and His Orchestra. Chrissie listened to the music and dreamed alternately about Ronald Ward and Lieutenant Kiely. Geraldo filled her with the stupor of romance.

Chrissie ran to the phone when she heard that her father was on the line. "Dada, we had a lovely wedding! Dillie was beautiful. Father FitzGerald gave a very funny speech. Bobby's been asked to sing in *Maritana*. Isn't that brilliant!"

"Doesn't he have a gramophone record of that?"

"He's the youngest person *ever* to be asked to take the lead at the Dungarvan Society."

"Tell him he should listen to the gramophone record."

"We're listening to Geraldo."

"Well, tell Bobby..."

"Oh, about eighty lengths of half-inch round iron went on sale in Macroom," Chrissie said suddenly. "Ned was worried about driving to Macroom. But he said that the supply side is desperate at the forge."

"Will you tell Ned to telephone me here." The Deputy was always keen to get his hands on scrap iron for fabrication. There was a terrible shortage of metals. Even Dublin Corporation had to curtail its flat-building programme because of the iron shortage.

"I will, I'll tell him that! I'll tell Mama to tell him." Chrissie could hear the Geraldo music gathering speed as Bobby wound the gramophone. She wanted to get back to the music. "Have to go. I don't like to leave Alice alone with Bobby. She's been very shy these last few days."

"You do that," the Deputy said, wishing that he was at home. "You keep her away from that brother of yours."

"He wouldn't hurt a fly."

Adele reclaimed the phone from her daughter. She was infected by the good humour of the music. "Isn't it wonderful about Bobby? To be asked to take a lead part!"

"Wonderful," he said. "I hope he's doing his work at the forge."

"He is of course. Don't you worry," she said. "And don't worry about this IRA thing. Don't put yourself out on a limb. They are such sinister people."

"That's a change, coming from you. I thought you were very sympathetic."

"They *are* rather sinister, aren't they, love?"

"We killed each other during the Civil War. I hate to see us going through the same rigmarole. Death is always a seed of bitterness. We should forgive, forgive, forgive. It's the only way."

"You're too good for that place," she said affectionately. "That Dáil is full of mean creatures."

"I don't give up."

ช

As July progressed, the Deputy became more and more despairing of the Taoiseach's attitude to the IRA. At the time groups of Republican prisoners went on hunger-strike. There was agitation and unrest in the detention centres. The condemned youth from Dungarvan was almost forgotten, buried along with the taboo subject of Republican protests. An independent deputy, Oliver J Flanagan, and Mr Norton of the Labour Party pleaded for the release of the Republicans on hunger-strike on humanitarian grounds. But the Minister for Justice replied that the hunger-strikers could have their liberty only if they obeyed the law of the state. He said that since the previous September two more guards had been murdered and that ex-internees were suspected. "I remember the last time we released a hunger-striker, he was a friend of mine," the minister said. "That unfortunate man was on the point of death, but inside a couple of months he and his comrade shot two of our guards in Rathgar and he had to be shot for it."

A few days later the Deputy returned home. He preferred to face the Old IRA commandant and the condemned man's family than listen to Dev. Their dependence on him put a great strain on his life. Dublin had begun to fill up with thousands of Ulstermen, Catholics who always flocked south to avoid the annual twelfth of July Orange celebrations. He was sorry for the Ulstermen who were caught up in a war that had nothing to do with Irish interests.

While sitting in the train he read *The Irish Times* and the *Irish Press*. He treated himself to the glut of news: he found news that didn't involve hunger-strikes very relaxing. One could bask by the sea of facts. The newspapers had abandoned the crisis created by the general election. It was now thought likely that there wouldn't be another election and that Dev would remain as Taoiseach until the end of the war. Instead the papers were full of news from southern Europe. There were inspiring accounts of the two thousand ships that had carried the Allied invasion troops on to the Sicilian shore. There was a report that the Polish premier and his commander-in-chief had died in an aircraft crash. He had been warned not to take the flight. Another example of a leader not listening.

"Rather tragic about the poor Polish prime minister." A man who was sitting opposite in the compartment seemed to read his mind. The man was prosperous-looking. He carried a brown hatbox as well as a leather suitcase.

"He was told not to go."

"One gets caught up in things, I suppose," the man

replied. "One becomes immune to advice. He should have taken a holiday."

"Are you on holidays yourself?"

"Indeed. I'm spending the next six weeks in Bally-bunion, that charming Kerry spa."

The Deputy hadn't thought of Ballybunion as an upper-class spa. He wondered why a gentleman needed a top-hat there. He glanced at the hatbox. "I see you are curious," the man spoke again, amused.

"I just wondered if there was a big dress-dance or some-thing in Ballybunion."

"Not at all." The man laughed. He had extraordinary, wolf-like, discoloured teeth. "I am an illusionist. A magician."

"I'm afraid I'm only a TD. A Dáil deputy."

"Ah, the supreme illusionist! A politician!" the man suggested, bowing his head in homage. "Which branch of the national entertainment society?"

"Fianna Fáil."

"Ah good, at least you are not a freemason. Would you like a boiled sweet?"

The Deputy hesitated and then took what looked like a sweet from a brown paper bag. "I trust this won't explode."

"You never know," the magician smiled.

The Deputy took up the *Irish Press* again and started to read. He sucked the boiled sweet cautiously. He expected something to happen. Then the magician tapped his knee. "I wonder could I borrow your *Irish Times*?"

"Of course." The newspaper was sprawled on the seat beside him. He gathered it up and gave it to his fellow passenger. It was quiet in the carriage, apart from the clatter of the rails. After a while a strange murmur filled the train, a rising and falling tide of female voices. "Oh, damn, we are stuck beside a convent of sisters. Nuns! I can't stand them! It will be rosary, rosary, rosary all the way to Limerick Junction."

"We'll just have to suffer it."

"No, I couldn't. I just couldn't. We'll get them moved."

"Some hope," the Deputy laughed. "They are camped there for the duration."

"Are you afraid of beetles, big black beetles?" the magician asked.

"Not at all," said the Deputy.

"Bear with me, my good man."

The magician went into a kind of trance. Beads of sweat appeared on his forehead. "The only beads I can endure," he said suddenly, before re-entering the trance-like state. Beetles began to appear on the floor, horrible black creatures. Soon there were beetles on the windows, the ceiling, crawling on the hat-box, lodging between the pages of the newspapers, falling when the Deputy turned the page.

"That's a lot of beetles," said the Deputy," How do you do it?"

"You should see the infestation in the neighbouring carriage."

There was silence. The praying had stopped. Then pandemonium. Screams, high-pitched screams, shuffling. Two nuns appeared out in the corridor of the carriage, shaking violently. "Close the door," the magician said. "Or we'll be overrun." More screams. Two conductors appeared.

Suitcases were thrown onto the floor. A young nun was carried away. An older nun, the natural leader, complained bitterly to one of the conductors. The word "move" was mentioned. The compartment door was slid open by a conductor.

"This carriage appears to have an insect infestation. They bite. We can accommodate you in a different part of the train."

"Not at all," the magician said. "Things are not too bad here." He looked at the Deputy. The Deputy said that he was prepared to stay put.

"Peace at last," the magician said.

"Where did you learn to do that?" asked the Deputy, watching as the beetles seemed to go rigid. Then slowly they began to disappear.

"Oh, my people have always had to use magic, even in the East End of London. Magic has prevented my cousins in Poland from being gassed to death. The trains were all derailed for a weekend."

"And then what happened? Did they escape to England?"

"Many got away. Many went east towards Uncle Joe."

"I see. It is hard being a Jew."

"Your powers of understatement are quite magical," the stranger said. "But you are curious about my cousins in Poland, yes?"

"Yes, I am. I have Jewish friends. I'm in the metal business, as well as politics."

"My cousins," the magician went on, "escaped from Hitler disguised as a flock of sparrows. They settled finally on the trellis in the rose garden at Regent's Park."

"I've always considered you to be God's chosen," said the Deputy. "By God, you are entitled to a bit of magic."

"You are too generous. May your boiled sweet last a fortnight."

CHAPTER FOURTEEN

The magician's boiled sweet was still in the Deputy's mouth later that evening when he tackled Bobby about the theft of petrol from the forge supply. It was Ned Kenny who insisted that Bobby had stolen it. Adele didn't believe him; she said that the two metal apprentices who claimed to have seen him taking petrol were just trying to have him removed from the yard. They didn't want him around because he was a careful supervisor. Her response only irritated Ned, who replied that Bobby had been using his BSA as well as the Manx-Norton. It was a scandal to see Bobby around the place on his machine while priests and doctors had their allowances cut.

The Deputy didn't take too kindly to the news. In fact, Adele regretted telling him. But she had to; otherwise Ned Kenny would spill the beans. Better for the Deputy to hear it from his wife. "Honest to God, that boy has gone to pieces these last few months. To think that he was going to be a priest only a year ago. What got into his head? Tell me, what is it? What's wrong with him? He didn't do a stroke to help me during the election campaign. He went off gallivanting with Alice one day. I was dead worried that he'd done something to the girl. He'll get an earful when I see him."

"Take it easy, now. You know how Bobby goes into a sulk if you're too hard on him."

"I'll give him sulks, I will. As if I hadn't enough on my plate. Tomorrow I have to go to Dungarvan to tell a poor woman that her son is going to be hanged. Hanged! Hanged by the Dáil! Can you imagine that, hanged by an Irish court, and no reprieve. I have that on my mind. It's destroying me. And what does my son do? Steals petrol!"

"If you're going to be too upset, I'll handle this myself," Adele said calmly, firmly. "I don't want trouble. I hold everything together while you're above in the Dáil. Don't go ruining the peace in this house."

"This house? My house!"

"Ah, come on, love, sit in here with me. Sit awhile. We'll work out what we should say to him."

But before they had a chance to move out of the hallway, Bobby and Alice came in the door, laughing. Alice, especially, was full of mirth. But when she saw the look on the Deputy's face she stopped dead, as if electrocuted.

"Alice, would you run along inside to Chrissie. She's in the kitchen. Bobby, come in here, please." Adele pointed to the sitting-room door.

"Right, Mama," he said, perplexed.

Once inside the room, out of Alice's earshot, the Deputy didn't waste time. "What the hell were you doing, stealing petrol from our yard supply? Are you a fool or what?"

"What's this all about? Calm down, Dada."

"I will not calm down. You know we live in a small town. By now every man jack knows that you've nicked petrol from the yard. And those that don't know will soon know. You can be sure the Fine Gael crowd will be mouthing about it. They'll probably say that I gave you the petrol. And the parish priest above in his house has had his petrol allowance cut! What got into you?"

"I took only a pint, not more than a pint."

"For God's sake, man, is your brain dead or what? How are the locals to know you took only a pint? Have you done a study? There's a war on. We've barely enough petrol to get us through this year, never mind the rest of the war. Of course what you need is more important than the whole country. You've become so selfish, you have..."

"We're just very upset, you can see," Adele interjected. She didn't want too many harsh words spoken. Her husband would be gone back to Dublin on Tuesday and she would have to repair the damage.

"Too selfish. And that goes for Alice too. You've been teasing that poor girl and her father depending on us to keep her safe until he comes back. Have you any sense of responsibility? Alice's family is Jewish. Do you know what that means? Thousands of her people have been murdered and imprisoned. We can't do much for those people, but by God, we can mind one soul while this war is on. Can't we do that? Can you control yourself? Can you?"

"I'm fond of Alice. Her real name is Asya. I'm very fond of her, and she has a lot of time for me."

"Dear God," muttered Adele. "I knew nothing about this."

Bobby looked at his mother. With his eyes he appealed to her for support, shelter from his father's onslaught. Anything.

"Look, you stay away from that girl. Treat her with respect like a sister. Chrissie has got on very well with her, but you...you have to go and treat her like a loose woman. Well, you'll have to stop."

"I won't stop."

"You'll get out of this house if you don't stop acting like a child."

"Now, there's no need for that." Adele restrained the Deputy but it was too late. Bobby burst into speech.

"Well, that's high humour, coming from you. Get out of the house. Who has been the man of this house since you took off to the Dáil ten years ago? Where were you when the younger ones needed a father? How many times have you forgotten Emer's and Runan's birthday? How many times?" There were tears in Bobby's eyes. He moved to the door of the sitting-room. "Hypocrite!" he cried. "Shedding woman's tears for the murderer of a policeman, a bloody IRA type, and no time for your own children." He slammed the door as he left the room.

Adele was angry with her husband. "You shouldn't lose your temper. You never lose your temper in public, so why lash us with it?"

"We can't have him turning into a thief and interfering with Alice."

"They're young. Have you forgotten what it's like to be so young?"

"That's why it's so dangerous."

"It won't come to anything. Alice is a sensible girl."

The Deputy sat down on the couch beside the gramophone. "I give up on that boy."

"What have you given up? I mean to say, what have you put into him?"

"Ah, Adele, don't *you* start."

The hall door banged. "I wonder where he's off to. He wouldn't do anything stupid, surely?"

"A bit of fresh air won't do him any harm," the Deputy said. He pulled a magazine from the rack by the couch. "Where did this come from? It's a copy of *The Bell*. The only man I've ever met who reads it is Paddy Little. He has a stack of *Bells* and *Capuchin Annuals* in his office."

"Do you think we could go for a walk ourselves?"

"Why not! Why not go right now?" the Deputy said. He dropped *The Bell*, but forgot to ask again how it came to be in their magazine-rack. It was Alice who had brought it into the house. She had wanted Chrissie to read an article by Peadar O'Donnell called "Cry Jew."

"We'll go then." Adele walked to the door, but before she reached it there was shuffling in the hallway. It was Ned Kenny. He had let himself in. "Ah, Ned," Adele commented, "you didn't knock?" Then she stuck her head back into the sitting-room. "It's for you," she whispered to the Deputy. "The informer."

"I've put the receipts and invoices in order like you told me." Ned stood nervously at the sitting-room door, not sure of his welcome.

"Come in, come in, man," the Deputy shouted. "Shouldn't you be at home now? You mustn't kill yourself with work."

"I only do as much as yourself," replied Ned. He wanted the Deputy to come to the yard to inspect the iron bars that had been brought from Co Cork. Ned wanted them to be sold as quickly as possible. At this time of year, before they got money for the harvest, farmers stopped buying things like metal cages, gates or coachwork. There were seasonal cash-flow problems. Ned thought that they could improve the cash situation by selling the iron as scrap to Dublin building firms. The Deputy took a long-term view. Metal was a valuable asset during the war. He wanted to hold that asset, and perhaps add to its value by cleaning and treating it.

"You're the boss; you know what's best," Ned replied wearily, like an old man.

"I do," said the Deputy. But he walked out to the yard with Ned. The walk with Adele was forgotten as the two men became absorbed in ledgers, invoices and cash-flow.

࣫

It was after midnight when Bobby returned to the house. Adele was in the sitting-room, waiting to talk. She intended to be serious, firm but affectionate. Alice was asleep in Chrissie's room. The three women, Adele, Alice and Chrissie, had talked for four hours about love and Bobby and military weddings and young doctors and the novel *Rebecca*. Adele felt strengthened by their talk. She had some of that strength left over. She wanted to pass it on to her son. She could hear that Bobby hesitated before passing by the sitting-room door. Then she heard his footsteps on the stairs, and a few minutes later the sound of his bed creaking. He had abandoned the day. She sat alone in the room for a long time, too weary to get up, sad but without tears. The Deputy was already asleep. She could hear his snores, those liquid trumpet sounds that announced to the world that the head of the family was in residence.

The Deputy rose early the following morning. Bobby was still in bed, so he didn't know whether he was tired or on strike. He took the battered train to Dungarvan. He walked from the station to the terrace of labourers' cottages. The condemned man's sister, the quiet girl with lovely legs, was scrubbing the doorstep. When she stood up he saw that she was wearing the same striped apron, only now it was dirtier with a small hole in the top left-hand corner.

"Deputy!" The girl was shocked to see him.

"Is your mother in?" he asked.

"I'll get her now. No, no, come on in, she's in the kitchen." He followed her in. The mother was sitting by the bulky wooden table with her son. They were trying to unravel a pile of snarled rabbit snares.

"They're always getting mixed up," the mother said. In the weak light of the kitchen her face looked even more sallow and furrowed. She wasn't surprised to see the Deputy. "Take a seat," she said coldly.

"I'm afraid it's not good news."

"I expected as much." The mother continued to fish

among the snares. "The old commandant warned us to expect nothing from you."

"That turncoat Dev is determined to kill off anyone who's for a real republic." The son's voice boomed across the little kitchen.

"It isn't as simple as that."

"What's simple?" the poor woman asked. "Is my own child's death something simple? Is Dev going to hang him? We may be simple people, but we're made in the image of our Saviour."

"He gave up the idea of hunger-strike when he learned that you were going to talk to Dev." The son stared at him savagely. A generation of frustrated politics blazed in his eyes.

"I didn't know that."

"God, but he's a cruel, cruel bastard," the mother wailed.

"He said he can't interfere with the process of the law. Not now."

"He has some cheek," the son replied. "Some cheek coming from a fellow who was in jail himself."

"I asked him to postpone the hanging, not to consider a date until I'd spoken to you."

Then the old woman broke down. Her face sank into the pile of snares on the table. The daughter moved to comfort her. When she raised her head again the snare-cords were glistening with the moisture of her tears, as if a snail had crawled across them. Not for the first time, the Deputy was struck by his own lack of power. He had the power to move nothing—he was just a messenger. How well the members of the Dáil had been named, Teachta

Dála, emissary of the Dáil. "You did nothing, so," the old woman cried. "You were our last hope. But you could do nothing. I prayed for you. I prayed for your intentions and for your family. Dev has left us with nothing."

"Ma!" her son tried to recall her from grief.

The daughter spoke quietly. "They've cut off our relief. We don't know why. My brother can't get any more money, and my mother's pension book hasn't been sent back to her. Why are they doing this to us?"

"Starving us and hanging us," the mother said. "May Dev rot in hell."

The son said, "Will you leave this house? You're not welcome. Leave this house, sir!"

"If I could do something...They can't stop your pension..."

"Go away now."

"Yes," the daughter said. "It's no good. Go away." She stroked her mother's matted hair and withered face.

The Deputy was surprised that the daughter didn't cry. Something had turned to stone inside her. He decided to leave. None of them made a move to accompany him to the door. When he reached the doorstep he halted. He could lessen their destitution. From the look of the snares he could see that the son wasn't much of a hunter. The family was actually hungry now. He could lessen that pain. He took four crisp pound notes from his pocket and returned to the kitchen. They looked on silently while he placed the money on the mantelpiece. "Missus," he said quietly," I'm going to look into that matter of your pension, that's not right. This is something to tide you over."

The dour son rose from his seat. "Dev's pieces of silver," he shouted. "Take it back. We don't want it. Blood money!"

"Sit down," his mother said.

"Take that money back!" He brushed if off the mantelpiece with his red fist.

"Sit down!" the mother repeated. The son backed away.

The Deputy sweated with panic. "It's not charity, ma'am. It's to tide you over. I've been broke myself. This has nothing to do with Dev or the Party."

"Thank you, sir. I know you're as helpless as ourselves."

"I am," he admitted. "I am, missus."

He left the house quickly. But the daughter followed him to the door. She thanked him for the money. "Dev has turned into a Hitler," she said. "It's so sad for Ireland."

"He's not as bad as that."

"He is," she insisted. "But thanks for the money. It's an awful lot of money. I don't think I ever saw four pounds together. Tomorrow is my father's anniversary. We had no money for a Mass."

The Deputy was shocked. "Say a prayer for me," he said. "I'm not going to give up." He walked away with his hands in his pockets, like a labourer who had failed to get work. His head drooped. He had a pain in his chest. He would have a three-hour wait for the train.

"Thank you," she shouted after him.

On his way to the railway station he saw a creamery lorry from Ballinamult parked at the roadside. He hitched a ride. He shared a cab with a west Waterford councillor who was embarrassed to be caught hitching a lift. At that time there was a lot of public disquiet about councillors' expenses and travelling allowances. Far more disquiet about that than about the deaths of young IRA men in prison. "Is there a drop of tea in that flask?" the Deputy asked, pointing to a raffia grocery bag.

"There is, you're lucky," the councillor replied. He reached for the flask and poured the Deputy a measure of lukewarm tea into a soiled cup.

"Thanks." The tea steadied his nerves. He couldn't help thinking about the old woman, her daughter with beautiful legs, her son with all that rage. And he thought about the cruelty of political interests, how those interests must run their course, even if it means the death of citizens, the death of vulnerable fanatics and misguided youth. He thought of the fanatical determination in the eyes of de Valera. There are moments, he said to himself, while the councillor yapped on about a pot-holed by-road near Lismore, there are moments when you know that almost everything is lost.

CHAPTER FIFTEEN

Then an amazing thing happened.

That was how Chrissie would begin her story of the late summer's day when she and Lieutenant Kiely sat on the warm creosoted planks of the steamer's quay below Cappoquin. They were waiting to watch Bobby's crew going through their paces (or "strokes"). "Here they come," Chrissie whispered when she saw the wafer-thin craft approaching from the boat-house end of the river. "Faster!" she screamed at Bobby and he roared back at her to shut up. The speed of the boat sent ripples across the tidal river; weeds swayed and drifted, and they could hear the gurgle of water under the worn planks of the quay.

"You're mad about your brother," the lieutenant said.

"Why shouldn't I be? He's the eldest."

"Maybe I'll get lucky like him." The lieutenant looked at her sheepishly.

"You are lucky," she said. "Don't we all love you?"

"Who's we all? Name them!"

"Me, for one," declared Chrissie, plunging into trouble. The waters of the tide lapped against the boards. She felt she was going to fall.

"That's great," he said. "We love you too!" He brushed back her thick hair and then held her head. They kissed, slowly and sensitively, but not passionately. The lieutenant was a timid man, and Chrissie wasn't yet sure of her judgement. "That was for love," the lieutenant said when they drew apart. Chrissie looked downriver to see if her brother had been looking, but the boat was now a black dot on the horizon. She could see the rhythmic flashing of the wet oars in the low evening sun. Bobby and his crew were moving very fast against the incoming tide. The tidal reach of the Blackwater went beyond Cappoquin, fifteen miles from the sea.

"What are *they*?" Chrissie asked suddenly. She pointed to four boxes that were bobbing in the water. They were a metallic, sparkling silver colour.

"Move back!" the lieutenant said in a panic. "They could be mines brought in by the tide."

"Oh, my God, Bobby's on the river!" Chrissie thought of the mine that had exploded and killed several people in Donegal. A few months before that a mine had floated up on the Blackwater tide and killed several cattle that were cropping the river-bank. On yet another occasion more than a hundred books had floated as far as the boat-house: among the books was a history of the American navy, a romance from the American Civil War, a copy of *Gone with the Wind* published by Macmillan of New York and the letters of Lindbergh, the aviator. Captain Mulvey had salvaged the lot, and the books were being pressed dry in his attic.

"No, it isn't a mine," the lieutenant said with relief. He lay down on the quay and stretched out his left hand. Chrissie went across to a clump of sallies and broke off a long sally rod. She returned to the lieutenant's side and together they coaxed one of the boxes under the quay. Because it was high tide, the box lodged between the water and the quay planks. Chrissie scrambled down to retrieve it. "There you are," she said with satisfaction. "Open it."

"We can't be sure about booby-traps."

"I'll open it, so. I'm not going to wait."

"All right, I'll open it." He prised off the lid with a knife. "God, that's fantastic," he said when he saw what was inside.

"Aren't they beautiful?"

"They're not Irish."

The box was stuffed with thousands of bone-dry ten-yen notes issued by the Central Bank of China. Chrissie took a thick wad of notes in her hand and shook them. "Money!" she shouted. "Money! Money!"

The lieutenant put a damper on her enthusiasm. "I wonder if we can claim them?"

"Of course we can. We found them, we dragged them in off the tide."

"I wonder what's in the other boxes?"

"Money as well, of course." Chrissie looked at her lieutenant, who was clutching several thousand yen. She kissed him and said it was a good omen. She looked impatiently in the direction of the southern horizon. Bobby would help them to get the other boxes that were tantalisingly out of their reach. She clenched her teeth.

"Come on, Bobby, come on."

"We may not be able to keep this money," the lieutenant warned.

"Don't be a spoilsport. We're going to be rich. We'll be rich together!" She spoke without thinking.

"I love you, Chrissie," the lieutenant said, overcome. A wad of notes slipped from his fist and sank in the water.

"They don't float. Isn't that magical?" said Chrissie.

Chrissie tried every tactic to hold on to their four silver boxes, even after they discovered that some of them contained beautiful ornaments and vases rather than money. Bobby and the lieutenant carried them to Alice's house, where they were supposed to be kept in secret, but Bobby couldn't keep a secret. Soon the whole family knew about the discovery. Chrissie then tried to spirit the boxes away from Alice's and hide them in the office of the ironworks. She was caught in the act by Ned Kenny, who said that she must report the find to the guards. "Would you ever stop interfering!" she screamed at Ned. But he was adamant.

Eventually, she did go to the sergeant of the guards, with Bobby. "There's no reports of Chinese ships being sunk off Youghal or Dungarvan," he said. "If you're lucky, nobody will claim these."

"They're mine. Ours," said Chrissie, for the thousandth time.

"You mustn't be selfish. Patience is everything in these times." The sergeant looked at her. "Was the lieutenant in uniform when these boxes were recovered?"

"He was not!" Chrissie could see what he was getting

at. If the lieutenant was on duty the boxes would automatically belong to the state.

The sergeant ignored Chrissie now and spoke to Bobby. "We must make a full list of all the contents. We'll have to keep them for a while to see if they are claimed. Wasn't there a sum of money, banknotes, in the haul as well?"

"No, there wasn't any money," she lied. "You're trying to take these boxes from me."

The sergeant was vexed. "Listen, you can have these things back if nobody reports them missing in the next few weeks. What use are foreign artefacts without the appropriate coupons? You can't retail goods without coupons."

Chrissie gave in. "All right, make your list. I want a copy of it."

They opened the boxes and spread the treasures across the long deal table in the sergeant's office. None of them had the vocabulary to name the things that their gaze fell on. There were various jewels and green statuettes, a seventeenth-century bowl, carefully wrapped, a small blue-and-white jar, twenty bars of American chocolate that had been purchased by an adoring father in the Yangtze delta, a silver ring with a marquise blue diamond, a cloisonné enamel tea-set, a black onyx and coral panther brooch and—wrapped in a page of the *Herald-Tribune* for August 1932—a small bronze medal, a souvenir of the Eucharistic Congress in Dublin, which had inscribed upon it: *Good luck to ye where e'er ye be. At home, abroad or on the sea.*

"There wasn't much luck going with the medal anyway," the sergeant commented. He rubbed the medal with a white

THOMAS M^cCARTHY

handkerchief that was grey with dirt. "It must have belonged to an Irish missionary."

"You can throw that thing away," Chrissie said.

"Everything must be left here." The sergeant put the medal up against the bare light-bulb. He was pleased when it sparkled.

"Lieutenant Kiely should have a copy of the list too," Chrissie suggested.

"You can share your copy with him."

After the formalities were completed they left the barracks. Chrissie held the list in her hand tightly, as if it were a primed weapon. When she met the lieutenant, he suggested that she put it away. "For God's sake, don't lose it," he said. They saw Alice in the distance. Chrissie shouted to her, although there was no need to shout; she was headed in their direction anyway.

"Did they take the treasures from you?" Alice enquired.

"They gave us a list. They'll have to give the boxes back to us if nobody makes a claim."

"I don't see why they should lock away *your* treasure. You have rights over your treasure trove. It's yours."

"I shouldn't have allowed Ned Kenny to panic me," said Chrissie. "He sounded so convincing. Honest to God, he's such an interfering young scut."

The four of them walked together to the Glenville house. By now the lieutenant was a familiar visitor and nobody took any notice when he arrived with Chrissie.

They walked into an argument between Adele and Ellie. Ellie, in slippered feet and Chrissie's woollen dressing-gown, was standing in the middle of the kitchen saying, "No, I mustn't take the money. I mustn't take it. I can't."

Adele was leaning against the sink, her sensitive fingers reddened from scrubbing. On the edge of the kitchen table lay an open envelope and eight pound notes placed beside it. It was the weekly wage that Adele had saved for Ellie during her long illness. But Ellie didn't want to take the money because she hadn't earned it. If anything, she felt that she owed money to the family. "I'm having no more old fuss about this. You'll take the money. You'll be getting married soon, so you'll have to save every penny." Adele returned to her scrubbing without greeting the four who had just come in.

"It is not honest. I don't deserve it."

"What's all this about?" Chrissie asked in a superior tone. Alice and the lieutenant, sensing Ellie's discomfiture, decided to leave before Ellie could answer. Chrissie saw them to the door and said a brief goodbye. Bobby slipped out after them as she returned to the kitchen.

"Fourteen shillings is little enough," Adele said, half-answering her daughter's enquiry.

"I should be paying *you*," Ellie said.

"You'll need every penny of it."

"I mustn't take charity."

"It's your pay, your pay."

"Even so."

Ellie raised her left leg to scratch her right shin with her slippered foot. It was a habit that infuriated Adele. It was so undignified. "I'm hearing no more about this," she said finally.

"Well, I'm not touching the money."

Ellie appealed to Chrissie but Chrissie took her mother's part. She said that Ellie had worked hard for years. She was like a member of the family but she worked and worked. She should look upon the money, which Adele had so carefully saved, as pocket-money. She had no opportunity to spend it because of her illness. And anyway, said Chrissie, introducing an angle that was completely irrelevant, how could she go on upsetting Adele? Why did she want to insult Adele, who had been so careful to save Ellie's money? That clinched it. Ellie looked mournfully at them. "I suppose I caused ye a lot of trouble. I won't cause any more. I'll take the money."

"Good woman," said Chrissie. "Now, no more of it, I'm starved."

"I know I don't deserve this money," Ellie wept.

"You'd never make a county councillor!" laughed Adele.

"I'll put on some decent shoes and help you with the tea," Ellie said, leaving the kitchen and scrambling up the stairs.

"That girl is full of foolish pride. All of that family is the same," said Adele. She felt slightly battered by the argument. While they stood in the kitchen she heard the evening paper, the *Evening Echo*, being dropped into the hallway. "Will you get that for me, Chrissie?" she asked.

Adele opened the paper in silence. After a little while Chrissie heard her say, "Oh, God!" in a whisper and, "God, your father will be so upset."

"What is it, Mama?"

"Look, Chrissie, look what Dev's done." There were tears in her eyes.

"What, what?" Then she found the news item. It was a government announcement that the young IRA man would be hanged on the fifteenth of August.

Adele clenched her fists in anger. "He is ruthless, isn't he, that bastard Dev?"

"There isn't an ounce of kindness in his heart," Chrissie said bitterly. "The Emergency has made him so black."

"The poor mother. What about the poor boy's mother? Dada's going to be heartbroken. I know he killed a policeman. But there's no need for this, more killing. Isn't there enough killing in the world? I've always kept quiet about Dev for your father's sake. I was a nurse in New York when he was strutting around the east coast. I always felt there was too much of the poet in him to trust his judgement. My father was the same. My father couldn't understand why your own father had so much time for him. My father always said that you couldn't trust a politician with Dev's uncertain social background."

"We must ring Dada," Chrissie said. "He'll be so lonely."

"After tea, yes, after tea we'll have to find him," Adele said. She folded the *Echo* and placed it on the press by the sink.

"I'll take that away; it'll get wet." Chrissie spoke in a sort of maternal voice. She had suddenly begun to practise maturity. Her young lieutenant and her Chinese boxes had come to her as a preliminary reward. Her life had begun to come into focus and she liked what she saw. "Do you know that Mr Healy is going to give Declan three shillings a week to walk his greyhounds?" she asked her mother.

"Declan never said anything to me. Now isn't that

typical!" Adele complained. Then, as if they might have been kidnapped, she said, "Where *are* all the children?"

"Don't worry, they'll be here soon. They'll smell the tea being made," Chrissie assured her.

"They are dirty animals—greyhounds..." Adele was interrupted by the roar of Bobby's Manx-Norton. They watched Bobby approach through the back-garden, his leather helmet, like the headgear of a fighter-pilot, still in place.

"I met Ned up town. He seemed very sour," he said when he entered.

"He doesn't like to see you on the public roads. He's sensitive about the petrol shortage," Adele complained. "And you should know that. Where did you get the petrol for today's ride?"

"How many fathers does a man need? It was the last drop left over since the day my own father insulted my integrity," explained Bobby. He walked across the kitchen, removing his helmet, and left.

"He really is a mechanical wizard," said Chrissie. "He could make that machine run on water."

"He could not!" Adele spoke angrily. "And don't you go defending him." She followed her son out into the hallway to tell him about the execution of the IRA man. If her son was to enter politics, and God forbid that he would, he should begin to follow current affairs.

While they were standing together in the hallway, Declan, Emer and Runan burst through the front door. "Is the tea ready yet?" Emer asked.

"Where's Gerald?"

Emer answered her mother. "He won't come away from the railway. He's just sitting at the cross and staring at the train. A goods train from Mallow has been derailed between the station and the river. Nobody knows why the train jumped between the tracks."

The family didn't wait for Gerald to come home. They all sat down and ate quietly until Adele brought up the hanging of the IRA man. This led to a discussion on the stupidity of the Republicans who were collaborating with the Nazis, the shortage of petrol, their father's meeting with Dev and the ownership of the Chinese boxes.

"Will the war be over this year?" Bobby asked.

"Not a hope," said Adele. "Sure the Americans are only making an impact now."

Bobby looked grief-stricken. "Soon there'll be no petrol at all."

"Is that all you think about? Honest to God..." Adele smiled at him.

"Pity we haven't petrol in Ireland. I mean in the ground," Emer said.

"Listen, girl, we can't even save the turf that we own. All the soldiers in the garrison have to spend their time saving turf. I heard it from Barry." Chrissie had great pleasure in saying his name.

CHAPTER SIXTEEN

"Try not to disturb your father," Adele said when Bobby mentioned that he wanted to try some pieces from *Maritana*, the musical he'd been asked to sing in at Christmas. His music was rusty so that sight-reading the light opera was a challenge. But he loved the challenge.

"You won't be doing it until Christmas. I don't know what all the fuss is about," complained Chrissie.

"Rehearsals start in September."

"Well, don't annoy your father. He has a lot of work to do."

But Bobby ignored her. He had been singing pieces from *Maritana* all weekend, ever since the Deputy came through the door, depressed and crest-fallen. The Deputy had sought another meeting with Dev but it was refused. Even Paddy Little was now too busy to see him. On his way into the sitting-room, Bobby saw the glass panel of the front door darkened by a male figure. He opened the door immediately. It was Lieutenant Kiely. "How are you, Barry!" he greeted the visitor.

The lieutenant spoke in a very officious tone. "I wish to

see your father." He was in full uniform. His buttons shone brilliantly in the pink light of the morning. His hair was combed neatly, plastered with hair-cream. He held his military cap in his left hand. But he didn't know there were two strands of straw on his right shoulder.

"There's straw on your shoulder," quipped Bobby. "A dead loss if you want to make an impression."

"Damn it!" The lieutenant brushed his uniform. "A donkey bolted when I was coming down the street," he explained. "It was pulling a load of straw, or was it hay? Anyway, it was startled by Coppertorn's dog. The whole street is covered with straw."

"Probably one of the old donkeys from the Civil War. They should be rounded up and slaughtered."

"I don't know." The lieutenant hesitated. "I would like to speak to your father, if you don't mind." He resumed his military posture.

"All right, all right. Keep your hat on," said Bobby. "There's nothing wrong, is there?"

"Nothing at all. I'd like to speak to your father."

"Jasus. Go in, so." Bobby opened the sitting-room door. "Dada, Barry here wants to have a chat with you."

"Who?" The Deputy was startled into rising from his chair. "Ah, Barry! Lieutenant. We never hear you called anything but lieutenant."

Bobby left the two of them and went back into the kitchen. "There goes my bloody *Maritana*. Lieutenant Kiely has just gone in to see Dada. He's acting very stiff."

"What! Barry's in with Dada! You fool!" screamed Chrissie. "I wanted to talk to him first." She stood up from the kitchen table. She was excited, terrified, thrilled. "Dada's in such a foul mood. He might *refuse*."

"Refuse what? It depends on what the lieutenant's looking for," Adele said calmly. "What *is* he looking for?"

"He's dressed to kill, anyway," Bobby commented.

"He's going to ask Dada if we can get engaged," Chrissie said triumphantly.

Adele was shocked. "You're only out of school. And his prospects are very uncertain. His battalion could be transferred anywhere. You must understand if your father says no, it's for your own good."

"If Dada says no, if he humiliates Barry, I swear I'll leave this house and you'll never see me again." Chrissie's face trembled with rage. Adele reassured her that they all liked the lieutenant, but said that even the fact that they still referred to him as the lieutenant rather than as Barry showed just how little they knew him.

"*I* know him," Chrissie replied. "*You're* not marrying him."

"Dada's in a savage mood ever since the hanging was announced. He'll eat your lieutenant alive," Bobby said.

Chrissie started crying. "Stop now," Adele said. "Look, we'll say three Hail Marys to give us all strength. To give Barry strength."

"To give me patience," said Chrissie.

Bobby didn't participate in this prayer session. He went back into the hallway to listen for the sound of blows, or at least the sound of the young lieutenant crying. The others prayed. From the hall he could hear the mumble of the women praying. Then, above all that, the sound of his father's laughter. "He must have thought he was joking," Bobby whispered to himself. He could hear his mother saying, "God give him strength."

Soon after that the sitting-room door was opened and the Deputy emerged, still laughing. "Come on, we'll tell the women." The lieutenant followed him, wearing his cap. He winked at Bobby. "Hear this!" shouted the Deputy through the kitchen door. "We'll have a doctor in the family. I always wanted a son a doctor."

Chrissie bolted towards her father.

"Chrissie and Barry are going to get engaged," the Deputy said to Adele, sounding surprised, as if this was the most amazing thing that had ever happened in his life.

"Barry, I'm so pleased." Adele embraced her future son-in-law. At that moment the lieutenant didn't think that she was very pleased; she seemed too reserved. Only years later would he discover what happiness he had brought.

"We should have a drink to celebrate," the Deputy said.

"We'll all have a cup of tea now," Adele spoke quietly, terrified that she might cry.

"All right, but after that the Railway Bar for a proper drink."

Adele kissed the young lieutenant on the cheek. "I'm truly glad."

"Isn't he just lovely?" Chrissie said to her mother. She hugged her fiancé.

"You're all lovely," the Deputy added. "We'll adjourn to the sitting-room, Barry. Let the women be wetting the tea. There should be a drop of whiskey or something in the press." He took the lieutenant firmly by the arm and dragged him along like a child. "Have you a voice?"

"What?"

"Have you any voice? Can you sing?"

"I'm afraid not," admitted the lieutenant. His first failure.

"Yerra, what harm. Bobby will give us a tune on the piano."

CHAPTER SEVENTEEN

Alice held her copy of the *Cork Examiner* to the light of the kitchen window. She was reading the grim account of the end of a BOAC flying-boat that had crashed into the slopes of Mount Brandon in Kerry. The flying-boat, lost and in trouble, had come down at four in the morning; it broke up, burst into flames and was destroyed immediately. Twisted wreckage and scarred bodies were left on the bracken and bog-water. The unlucky machine had left Liston carrying seven crew and eighteen passengers. Four miles from the place of the crash a blood-spattered member of the crew stumbled into the house of a man named Patrick Corkery. The scene of the crash was so isolated it was nearly twelve hours before the survivors reached Tralee Hospital. At least there were survivors, thought Alice. The little flying-boat absorbed into the indifferent mountain, like a drifting mine hitting a Donegal pier, was a perfect metaphor for the distant rumble of war. Little bits of conflict sheared off like pieces of metal and became embedded in the neutral land.

In her pocket, Alice kept a long letter that she had

received from her father from London the previous day. He was even more heavily engaged in "religious" work. He related some stories from the Axis occupied territories, terrible stories of mass murder. He wanted to know if she had heard Arthur Koestler's broadcast on the BBC about the death-trains. Some people thought that the account was a drama for radio and one of the famous Sitwells had written to congratulate Koestler on his wonderful imagination. The accounts that her father wrote stiffened her resolve. She was determined to get out of Ireland. Living in a neutral country tended to make citizens blasé about evil. Her father suggested that she cross to England in the autumn," preferably September." The danger of a German invasion had passed because of the successes of the Russians. Her father planned to leave London for Bath or Weston-super-Mare. If Alice learned typing she could help him officially, he said. She wasn't quite sure what he was doing. So far he had been involved in a committee for relief work in Bradford and London. He had visited an orphanage in Bath, and he had been to Glasgow and Liverpool. Whatever it was, it was covered by the euphemism "religious work."

Alice felt wasted in a small neutral town. Her friendship with the Deputy's family had kept her alive emotionally. The brief, unsought moments of excitement with Bobby had come at the point where she herself felt more hopeful about the war. By mid-1943 she knew that both she and her father's business interests in Ireland would survive. On top of this was the excitement of secret flirting. But even her real name was still kept hidden from almost everyone, an extraordinary feat. If she stayed put she would never become herself. She would always be an appendage to the Glenvilles.

She needed to talk to the Deputy, who was her surrogate father. She got ready and left her house to walk to the Glenvilles'.

On the street, two male voices called to her. Turning, she saw Mr Lincoln and Ned Lonergan.

"Hello, Alice, girl."

"Hello, Alice."

They too were going in search of the breakfasting Deputy. "Are you going to the big match tomorrow?" Ned Lonergan asked her. He was referring to the Munster senior hurling final at the Cork Athletics Grounds.

"I am."

"I suppose you'll be shouting for Cork!" said Mr Lincoln.

Ned Lonergan took her hand in a fatherly gesture. "You must shout for Waterford. Sure, you are one of our own now." So many fathers.

"Yes, I'm going with the Glenvilles. But I'm keeping the peace. I won't shout for anyone." Alice's mind was still full of details from the *Examiner*. She had seen the advertisement for Hedy Lamarr's new film *White Cargo*, which was showing in the Pavilion. That would be more fun than a hurling match. She felt for her father's letter in her pocket. She recalled as well the news item about the anti-Semite, Ezra Pound of Hailey, Idaho, who had just been indicted by the American government. The 57-year-old poet was among eight men and women who would be hanged for treason for broadcasting propaganda from Axis radio stations. News of the war was becoming more and more important to her. She was becoming a Jew again. How strangely irrelevant was Mr Lonergan's and Mr Lincoln's sporting enthusiasm. How far removed from everything that was vital to her. "I'll wear green tomorrow," Alice laughed. "Green for neutral."

ॐ

The Deputy was surprised by his early-morning delegation. "Am I a lazy hoor or have you all trouble sleeping?" he said. He looked up at Alice, ignoring the two men. "You're welcome, love. These two tinkers can have their breakfast elsewhere."

"I was up at seven," Ned Lonergan said proudly.

Mr Lincoln outbid him. "I was already at Mass."

"A repentant Republican. That's what the bishops like to see."

Alice handed him her father's letter. "It's all a bit sudden," she said. "All the plans will have to be made quickly."

"I was expecting that." The Deputy glanced briefly at the letter. He said that her father had been in touch with him and that he thought everything had changed. "Things can only get better."

"I wish that were true," said Mr Lincoln. "The food shortages are terrible. Soon I'll have nothing to sell in the shop."

"We're talking about England," explained the Deputy. "Alice, will you go in and say hello to Adele and Ellie. They're in the kitchen. I'll try to get rid of these two nuisances." He led the two men into the sitting-room. They had their own worries. The writ authorising the return of the successful deputies in the constituency, including the minister, Mr Little, had not been deposited with the clerk of the Dáil. The county registrar and Mr Colbert, the returning officer, had posted the writ to Dublin, but an empty envelope addressed to the clerk of the Dáil had been found at the Waterford sorting-office. It was assumed that the writ had been stolen, probably by Republican activists, in order to create chaos in the constituency. "I was speaking to Mr Colbert," the Deputy said," and he thinks that the *Aiséirí* crowd were trying to get at me because I failed to do anything about that IRA lad."

"Jesus, you did everything. You even got to Dev."

"I did sweet damn all." The Deputy shook his head. "I don't know how Dev can do this to us. Things will start going wrong when the IRA man is hanged. You'll see, small things like the bloody writ. They'll just make life miserable for us all."

Ned Lonergan said there might have to be another election if the writ weren't found. And if there were another election the party might lose a seat. "My seat," the Deputy added, but Mr Lincoln disagreed. It would be a Farmers' candidate who'd lose out, he suggested, because a lot of farmers wouldn't give another day to voting, travel and all that. They would still be in the thick of the harvest.

"Don't change anything," Ned advised. "You must function with confidence. You've got a session in Dungarvan on Monday morning and that meeting about the bakery strike in Kilmacthomas on Monday night. You have to turn up at those things."

"I must go to the IRA man's hanging," the Deputy said suddenly. He took a ball of paper from his pocket and unravelled it. The paper was sticky with saliva and black dye. It was the remains of the magician's boiled sweet. He put the pieces in his mouth.

"Stay away. That would be my advice," Mr Lincoln said.

The Deputy spoke with the sweet still in his mouth. "No, I want to be at Mountjoy when the lad is hanged. His family need our support. It's my bloody duty to be there."

"'Bloody' is an unfortunate word," said Mr Lincoln.

"Mr Colbert said he'd ring me again."

"What?"

"About the writ! The writ!" the Deputy said.

"I'd advise you to stay away from the IRA lad's hanging. Nothing can be gained from it," said Mr Lincoln.

"I have to go. He is my constituent; his family needs the support."

Mr Lincoln was adamant. "Support! If you arrive outside the prison they'll see it as a provocation. I'm telling you, they will."

"Please God, it'll pass off without trouble," Ned Lonergan said hopefully.

"It depends on the Republicans," the Deputy replied. "They might want to exploit the situation. They have another Kevin Barry in that lad. But that's not going to keep me away."

"As long as you keep your distance," Mr Lincoln said.

"I will, I will." The Deputy thought again about Alice

and her father's letter. What news had she brought of the outside world, what were her plans? He wondered if he could get rid of the two Party men. But they expected to make a morning of their visit. They had no intention of going away. "We'll go in and see what we can do for Alice," he said, finally reconciled to their presence.

CHAPTER EIGHTEEN

The following day a large crowd gathered at the railway station to catch the train to Cork. It was a sea of blue and white; women wore blue dresses and men carried hastily made blue-and-white flags. When the train pulled in, it seemed already too full. Youths with red faces and watery eyes leaned out of windows and waved the county colours. After the crowd had inserted itself, the train, blue and gasping like an asthmatic, pulled away laboriously. Alice and Captain Mulvey and all the Glenvilles except Runan and Gerald were aboard. They scrambled through the narrow passageways. They were disgorged at Glanmire station after an uncomfortable three-and-a-half-hour journey, stiff-limbed and covered in perspiration. "That train was over-crowded," the Deputy said. It was hardly a brilliant observation.

"You'd never get away with that kind of crowding on a steamer," Captain Mulvey announced. But Alice said that in India people sat on the roofs of trains.

"If that is so," replied Captain Mulvey in a tone of reprimand," if that is so then there can't be pigeons in

India. If you tried to sit on a roof in Ireland you'd be covered in bird-droppings."

Alice wanted to let the matter drop, but the captain went on. It was practical considerations like that, he said, that determined the character of a culture. They walked on in silence, considering the captain's wisdom. There was still two hours to go before the game. Bobby, Alice and Chrissie planned to visit the agricultural exhibition in the university grounds. Their detour would kill an hour at least. "I'll see where Barry studied to be a doctor," Chrissie said enthusiastically. "He said he'd meet us at the clock-tower, or was it the stone corridor? Which did we decide?" she asked Alice.

"They're both just off the quad. We won't get lost, don't worry."

He was standing under the stone arch of the clock-tower. It was Alice who recognised him first. Chrissie was short-sighted, and getting worse. "My God, but you're a picture," she said to him. The lieutenant was in mufti, wearing an outsize cardigan and a green tie that looked like army issue. Alice thought he looked ridiculous and middle-aged, but Chrissie was enthralled. "We brought sandwiches," she said. "I thought we could have a picnic at the exhibition."

"We can forget about that," he said.

"What's wrong?" Bobby was annoyed.

"They've closed down the main hall. They've all gone off to the hurling."

Everyone was disappointed but the lieutenant tried to cheer them up. "Lots of places to have a picnic," he said.

He moved to embrace Chrissie, and they kissed self-consciously. "I must show you where I went to lectures," he said. "Well, I'll show you the Pathology Department." They walked together along the quad, the lieutenant pointing out and naming various university buildings. "That," he said, pointing to a tall gate that barred the entrance to the exhibition field," that is where the agricultural show is impounded."

"We'll climb over," Bobby suggested.

"No," said Chrissie.

Bobby laughed at that. He said that her sense of adventure was fading. He ran along the perimeter of the exhibition garden, rattling the fence and testing the posts. But nothing would give. "You can take the man out of the bog..." said Chrissie. "Would you look at him? He thinks he's badger-baiting."

Finally Bobby gave up. "We may as well have that grub," he suggested, "or we'll be late for the match."

They walked along to a river-bank that was covered with laurel and camellia bushes. They found a break in the dense mass of greenery and sat down.

"The coffee is disgusting." Bobby complained.

"It's the substitute stuff. What do you expect?" Chrissie answered his complaint. "There's a war on, you know."

"Thanks." Bobby finished his sandwich. He looked up at Alice, who smiled back at him boldly and mischievously. "So you're going away. I can't believe you're going to go to England."

"I don't know what I'll do without you, Alice," said Chrissie. "You're the only friend I have."

"It'll be lonely. Miserable," Bobby said with emphasis.

Alice looked at him and scrutinised his face lovingly. "It will be miserable going away." She kissed Bobby. This surprised him so much that he spilled his blue cup of coffee. Alice looked at the lieutenant and Chrissie, slightly embarrassed. "I think we all hide our feelings too much," she said, trying to read their minds.

"That's the way life is," Chrissie said, with all the philosophical wistfulness of someone secure. She held her fiancé's hand like a girl holding the reins of a pet pony. The four of them looked at the river, which was starved of water because of the summer drought. A family of coots fussed across the water close to the other bank. Two long, thin, domestic cats hopped through the tall grasses that grew between the backyards of the terrace of houses on Western Road. Bobby clapped to startle them, but they paid no heed to that. Too many students had already tried to frighten them.

"Sensible cats," said the lieutenant.

"They are probably deaf," Bobby suggested. "Deaf from the noise of the city." He lay back on the grass so that his head touched Alice's thigh. He pressed a little closer when she didn't move away. Alice didn't stir, but rested on her right elbow in a half-sleep. The air became ripe with sexual possibilities, blood warming with the early afternoon. Two cats in the distance were like sparks of sexual energy, coiled and playing. Chrissie settled down to doze in the nest of her lieutenant's chest. They remained like that for over half an hour, their bodies stealing contact, a kind of adolescent contact that their more adult minds could deny if necessary.

"It's so quiet," Chrissie said eventually. "There's hardly any traffic."

"They are all at the match."

"The match, lads!" Chrissie jumped to her feet and started tidying up.

"Ah, we're too late. Let's stay here altogether," said Bobby. A moist layer of heat had developed between his head and Alice's thigh.

"We *can't* stay. Dada will want to know what we thought of the match. We can't waste four tickets. There'd be murder back in Cappoquin if people found out that we'd wasted four tickets."

But when they reached the Athletics Grounds the match had already begun. The gates were shut. "Let us in!" Bobby shouted at a man with a red face who was leaning against one of the bolted entrances.

He ignored them.

"We've come all the way from Waterford. You must let us in!" Alice pleaded.

"Go back to the bog!" the man shouted above the roar of the crowd. He turned to his companion and refused to look at them.

"That's terrible," Bobby complained. "Dada will be furious that we wasted the train fares." The two women turned their backs to the gate and watched a group of street-traders tidying their stalls. One tall thin man rolled up a long red curtain, revealing two upturned tea-chests that had served as a shop-counter.

"I've an idea," Alice shouted. "We'll buy the tea-chests

from that man over there."

"I'm not standing on any tea-chest, I'd break my neck," said Chrissie.

"Not with your hard neck surely," said Bobby. He walked across to the trader and offered the man two shillings for the two boxes.

"Five bob," the man demanded.

"Ridiculous. Daylight robbery!"

"Your need is my profit," the trader said.

"I haven't got five bob. Look!" Bobby pretended to search his pockets. "I've only got two bob! My father's a Dáil Deputy. He's inside there with all my money."

"A politician! Huh! He's in there with all my money as well. Use your political skills to rob three shillings from your companions."

"Half-a-crown."

"Look, three shillings, then." The man looked like he needed to get to a lavatory.

"Half a crown."

Then they heard the crowd cheering. Cork had scored a goal. "We're missing it all. I'll give you sixpence to put with it," Chrissie said. She had no particular interest in sport, but she hated to be left out of anything. The two tea-chests were handed over without further ceremony. Alice and Chrissie stood on the boxes nervously while the two men held their thighs.

"Come on, Waterford!" shouted Chrissie. Now that she could see the players her parochial pride came to the fore. Alice wasn't that interested in the match. Hockey was her game. But she gave the others a terrible fright when she nearly leaped from the box at one point. Cork had scored yet again.

"You can have a look now," Chrissie said to Barry. But he wouldn't hear of it. He said she wasn't to worry about him. His hands were gripping her thighs firmly: they were protected from his sweating hands only by the light fabric of her dress.

Waterford lost the match. The disappointment of the four was mitigated by the long game of touching that they had played. Afterwards, on the train, they teased the Deputy about the defeat.

"It's all right for you lot," he said. "Sure half your quartet is from Cork."

"No jealousy," the lieutenant replied.

"Bigger county. The biggest county in Ireland. It's easy for them to get a team together."

The lieutenant wouldn't let that go. "Ah, well, it has to do it with style too, with flourish." He looked at Chrissie for approval. When it wasn't offered he shut up. After twenty minutes they all fell silent; the rhythm of the carriage and the closeness of bodies was relaxing and soporific. The Deputy was on the point of nodding off when a thin-faced man in an elegant suit stood over him. "All the seats are taken above. I wonder if I could join you?" he asked with extreme politeness.

"Yes, yes! Certainly!" The Deputy nudged Alice, who had fallen asleep. "Push in, Alice!"

"Very grateful," the man said. He looked prosperous but he was carrying only a book. "My case," he said, "is gone ahead of me on the 6.30 train. I was so engrossed in my book that the train pulled away. They've telephoned Dungarvan station to have it held."

"A nasty shock," Captain Mulvey mused, "to lose one's luggage. I remember once missing a ferry for Gibraltar. Very nearly went AWOL."

"You were a sailor?" the man asked. He cradled the large book in his lap. Alice, now wide awake, eyed him suspiciously. Was he a German agent?

"Merchant marine for many years," the captain said proudly.

The man nodded and opened his book. He was dying to get back to it.

"You're on your way to Dungarvan?"

"Yes, I'm an accountant." The man smiled.

"Keeping up with the trade, then," the Deputy pointed to his book.

"Afraid it's only a novel," he apologised. "By a Dublin-man, a fellow called Joyce."

"A West of Ireland name," Captain Mulvey said.

"Indeed." The accountant opened his book again, dismissing the company. A postcard fell from the book and dropped at the Deputy's feet. Alice reached down to pick it up and as she did so noticed that the writing was in German. A Berlin scene. She froze in terror. He was a spy, surely.

She nudged the Deputy to draw attention to the card.

"You've been abroad?" enquired the Deputy, handing him the card.

"Oh, a long time ago. That card, that card from Berlin, was one I sent my father in Clonakilty, I was on a hiking tour with my English cousin."

"There won't be much left of Europe," the captain said. "Not after all the Allied bombing. You were lucky to see Germany before this terrible war."

"You're a Corkman?" asked the Deputy. "What brings you to these parts?"

"I'm trying to reorganise a mineral water company. It has been bought by my family. My name's Hurley. My firm's name is Deasy, though. Where do you hail from?"

"Cappoquin. Cappoquin on the Blackwater."

"Fancy that," said Mr Hurley. "Cappoquin on the Blackwater. That very town is mentioned in this book."

"No!" They all sat up on hearing that.

"Is it a local history?" enquired the Deputy. "I'm surprised the author hasn't been in touch with me."

"Oh, he's trapped, trapped on the continent. Come to think of it," Mr Hurley went on, "he died a couple of years ago." He went back to his book.

They watched him furtively, but he seemed completely absorbed in what he was reading.

CHAPTER NINETEEN

There was a crowd standing outside the gates of Mountjoy Prison. A few minutes before, just after eight o'clock, a notice had been pinned to the gate to announce the execution of the young Republican. The notice, signed by the governor, was read aloud by a middle-aged man in a grey trench-coat. He stood back from the gate and led the crowd of about seventy people into a decade of the rosary.

Suddenly, the distraught mother turned on the Deputy. "Curse you! Curse you, you'll lose what I lost!" she screamed. "Oh God, oh God, oh God!" She struck the Deputy and spat in his face. Her quiet daughter, dressed in black rags, face deeply furrowed with grief, moved to restrain her.

"I swear to you, ma'am, I did everything I could."

"You did nothing for us!" her son accused him. The crowd continued to pray.

"I met Dev. I got as far as Dev. I went over the minister's head."

The son went on. "You made no public plea. You had your moment during the election. You made no public statement. You could have saved my brother, you bastard!"

The Deputy looked at him angrily. Anger had replaced fear. "I can't embarrass my Party. Not in this time of war, not now. You know that."

"If you were a man you'd stand outside your Party! But no, you wouldn't stick your neck out. You wouldn't risk your skin even for a human life!"

"Stop it, stop!" the quiet daughter said. She turned to the Deputy then, to protect him, he thought. But, instead, the words she spoke chilled him to the core. She spoke quietly. "Don't think we'll forgive you," she said. "We have longer memories than that. We know where your money came from, where you got the money for your business. It was Republican money. We haven't finished with you yet. As God is my witness you'll pay for your cowardice."

The distraught mother handed her a rosary. "May Jesus and His Blessed Mother forgive them," the mother said. "Them and their Dáil that killed my child. That gave the rope to an English hangman."

"I swear I did what I could. An election campaign is the worst time to plead."

"It's the best time! It was our only hope!" the daughter said.

The crowd prayed with all the fervour of the wounded, the dispossessed, the abandoned. They were the outcasts. "Go away!" the mother said to the Deputy. "Go away!" she repeated.

"Out! Out! Out!" the crowd chanted.

The Deputy acquiesced. The crowd became absorbed in a sorrowful mystery, their eyes turned to the notice of execution as if it were a holy picture. The dead man's sister watched the Deputy peel away from the crowd, like a ewe watching a wolf withdrawing.

He had attended. He was with his constituents. No Republican could condemn him outright. He had attended. He was the only Dáil deputy present.

&

He didn't have long to wait for distraction. The consequences of the IRA execution were forgotten in a new crisis at home. It involved Ellie's sister, Margaret, the girl who had nearly lost her job earlier in the year. She had been beaten up by her brother when the family discovered that she was pregnant. She had sought refuge in the local convent, where the Deputy visited her. She was pale and frightened and swollen-lipped. After five minutes of conversation she confirmed what the Deputy had already guessed. "It was Mr Cantwell. I'm not a loose girl."

"Does he know this?"

"Yes."

"Do you want me to speak to him about it? Your father and he should meet."

"No! No! The nuns will fix me up."

"I never liked Cantwell," the Deputy confided foolishly. "There was always something slimy about him."

"At first he just wanted to touch me, to put his hand up and feel me. I couldn't say no. I'd lose my job. But one Sunday when his family were at Mass he came into the room where I was making the beds. He wanted everything. He tore into me like a bull."

"You needn't tell me, child."

"I want to tell someone. What'll happen to me? My father hasn't come near me."

"That's where I can help. I'm going to your house with Ellie. We'll have a long chat with that father of yours."

"It'll do no good."

The Deputy said that she should wait and see. He smiled at her without condescension. She ceased to be pathetic after that, strengthened by her talk with someone familiar.

Although there were only a few hundred yards between the red-brick terrace where the Deputy lived and the labourer's cottage that was Ellie's family house, the Deputy was in unfamiliar territory. Ned Lonergan usually canvassed that area. He was shocked by the living conditions in the house. Ellie and her sister had been born into a family of seasonal agricultural labourers, the most brutalised and humiliated class in the country.

The Deputy and Ellie stood at the door while the father stirred himself from an asthmatic slumber. The room was dark. They had a single wall-lamp that had gone out two weeks before because of the shortage of oil. The only source of light was two four-inch stubs of candle, kept for emergencies. A small fire spluttered in the earthen grate; it had been stacked with freshly cut lime logs from the commonage by the river. A blackened teapot was simmering on the hob. The Deputy soon discovered that the whole family slept in one room that was really only an open balcony. If he had been curious he would have discovered that the downstairs bedroom was devoid of furniture, containing only a tattered fishing-net that had been nailed to the wall for repair. Looking down the dark hallway towards the rear he could see great chunks of light coming through holes in the back door. He looked again. It wasn't just a hole in the door but a hole in the floor where rats had gnawed through the weak concrete mixture.

"My father," Ellie said when the man rose to greet them.

"Deputy Glenville," the man greeted him.

"I came about your daughter."

The smile left the man's face. "A brazen bitch. She's no daughter of mine. None of these things ever happened in my side of the family." He pointed to Ellie. "Now, there's a good girl. More like my side of the family. Her mother's crowd are an ignorant breed."

Ellie started to cry. "Look at that!" her father said. "Do you see how that other little bitch has upset her!"

The man's son spoke from an even darker corner. "Ellie's soft." This startled the Deputy, who hadn't noticed him. It was like the darkness speaking.

"They are both your daughters," the Deputy said sternly. But the father replied that Margaret was nothing to him. Nothing. She had disgraced the family. This made the Deputy's blood boil. He told them that the girl had been badly abused. As usual, he said, it was the girl who was made to suffer. He warned them to stand by the girl and not to let Cantwell off the hook. "There's no point in threatening to beat your own child, do you hear me?" He looked at the son with a particularly poisonous look. He was the one who had beaten her.

"What can we do?" the father asked. "Mr Cantwell is a respectable man in this town. His name is always in the top ten of the church collection. Half the farmers in this parish are related to him. We'd never get work again if we disgraced him."

"There are other jobs."

"Where? Where are the other jobs?"

"You must visit the girl."

The father pushed the blackened teapot closer to the fire. "You'll have a drop?" he asked. The Deputy prepared himself for the torture of reheated tea. God knows how many times they had already used the tea-leaves. Ellie moved to a battered green-painted cupboard to get two mugs. There was a long expectant silence while they tasted the contents of the pot. There was very little to say. Ellie was still angry with her violent brother and didn't wish to speak to him. Her brother was already too embittered by life to make polite conversation with a deputy.

The Deputy said, "I'm taking her with me to Dublin next week. I want you to visit her in the convent before she goes, do you hear me?"

"Thanks be to God she'll be out of the parish," the father said.

The Deputy repeated that the father should visit her. He said that he expected it. She would be put into a nice home until the baby was born. After that, the nuns would find her a job. "As for Mr Cantwell, he's another matter entirely. He shouldn't be allowed to get away with this. You can talk to my solicitor if you like. It's your own business, but he should pay something to your daughter. He's ruined her life."

"We'll see," the father said, without enthusiasm. He

could think only of the disgrace. If he could stop thinking about it it might go away. At least his daughter was being removed from the area.

When the Deputy returned to Dublin Margaret went with him. They took the early train so that few in the town noticed their departure. He brought her to a hostel in Drumcondra where he told them that she was a cousin of his. He thought that she would be better treated if they knew she was a politician's relative. He was proved right. After that he went back to other constituency work.

❧

What might have been a political crisis following the summer election was averted by the astuteness of Dev. There was a worsening in the supply situation due to the relentless suction of the Allies, who were gathering already for the major battles ahead. There was even a butter shortage. Creamery managers and department officials spent a hot August week comparing figures. The inquiry showed that cows had become lazier: milk yields were down. Lower milk yields led to a rise in the value of goats. Goat-smuggling became a major topic of conversation. The papers made much of a skirmish at the border between customs officials and bands of travellers who had tried to smuggle a herd of goats into the Six Counties. The Deputy also watched the scrap-metal market. He expected the minister to bring in an order to confiscate garden railings and park benches to provide raw material for construction. The Deputy had stockpiled a supply of metal tubes along with unsold gates and cribs and he stood to make a lot of money out of them if the metal crisis deepened.

The Deputy was relaxing in his flat, listening to John McCormack on his wind-up gramophone, when there was a knock on the door and a persistent ringing of the bell. He opened the door to Paddy Little, the minister from Waterford. "My God, is something up?"

"The writ. It's been found!" the minister said excitedly. "We're safe, thanks be to God."

"How did it turn up?"

"Seemingly there were two envelopes posted in error, one empty and one containing the writ. The empty one arrived first, wouldn't you know!"

"And we were all blaming the poor Republicans."

"He has a wonderful voice," the minister said about John McCormack.

"Golden," the Deputy agreed. "One of the few Irishmen with real talent."

ᘒ

Back in Co Waterford Ned Kenny came into the Glenville house in an angry mood. He had just seen Bobby take off on his BSA scrambler. He wanted to report this to Adele.

"A huge load of scrap has just arrived from Kanturk. We need all hands to unload it. Just when we need an extra pair of hands he goes off," complained Ned.

Adele twisted the gold wedding-ring on her finger. She was feeling tense, a prelude to a migraine. She thought Ned looked ridiculous in his clean shirt and tie. He always wore a bright tie under his overalls. She could never accept this image he wished to project, of the would-be manager.

"Did you not hear him starting up? Why didn't you stop him?"

"How could I hear him?" Ned replied. "The lads were shouting and one of the steam-trucks was in the yard."

"He's just unhappy at the moment. You must understand," Adele pleaded. "Alice is going away and he has no friends."

"Listen, if he helped the lads in the yard he'd have plenty of friends."

"He's just adventurous," Adele explained. And then, as if she suddenly resented Ned's interference, she said, "He can't abide boring people. He is a creative person."

"Well, he'll never be a politician. The Party couldn't depend on him."

"Let us worry about that," Adele said angrily.

Ned left the house, still angry. Someone in the yard would get an earful. Adele smiled. She couldn't decide whether she admired or pitied Ned. He was such a serious young man.

Chrissie and Alice came in after Ned left. "Where's Bobby?" said Chrissie. "We went to the yard to see if he was there."

"Gone. Off scrambling. There's no stopping him," Adele said.

"He's wicked, really wicked. Those bikes will have to be locked away."

"He'd never stand for that. He'd go crazy."

"Well, that's what the men in the yard are saying."

"They can say what they like. I'm his mother."

"He listens to nobody," Chrissie went on.

"I'm definitely going in October," Alice said. She had come to tell Bobby.

"What about your house?" asked Adele. "You don't want to leave it vacant, not through the winter."

"You won't believe this. Chrissie and I have solved the problem. We'll ask Ellie and Michael to move in when they get married. They'll be married soon. It's more convenient than the other place they had in mind."

"You trust them?"

"Of course," Alice replied with a quizzical look. "Why, should I not trust them?"

"There's no reason why you shouldn't," Adele replied. She looked out the window. They could hear the sound of a truck being revved and men shouting.

Adele jumped suddenly, as if bitten by an insect. "Oh. The devil has walked over my grave."

"What? What do you mean?" asked Alice.

"Something has happened. Chrissie love, will you go to the phone in the office. Stay there."

"Mama, you're so superstitious."

Adele was as white as a sheet. "Something has happened."

Something terrible *had* happened. At that moment Bobby's scrambler was upside down in the river, the front tyre showing above the surface like an otter's pelt. He had been scrambling along the railway embankment between the main road and the river. Long accelerated runs, the engine roaring, fumes pouring out. A huge black-and-white donkey, this one owned by Tom Fercombe, a local peddler, appeared from nowhere. Bobby swerved to avoid the beast and was thrown from the machine. He was hurled through the air at fifty miles an hour. The clinging rhododendrons might have broken his fall had not an old gaslight holder jutting from the bank caught his head. He was decapitated, his head dropping between the irons of the gaslight holder and his body catapulted into the bushes.

Twenty minutes before the telephone rang Adele was already in shock. The children thought it was a migraine attack. Their father, chatting with the Minister for Posts and Telegraphs, had placed another record on the gramophone. He had no sixth sense or intuitive links with the dead.

CHAPTER TWENTY

The Deputy lifted the window to breathe in the dry air of a fair day. It was another Thursday in Cappoquin. There was an aroma of dry straw. The street below the window was bathed in the orange light of early morning. Too many things have happened, he thought, too many things have come to a head or fallen apart, lost forever. Adele was still asleep. She had drained herself in two days of weeping. Her son was dead, her first-born who emerged like a phoenix from the ashes of the Civil War. The joy of the first-born is never lost. He heard the sound of vomiting from the bathroom. He guessed it must be Gerald or Runan: they had been drinking Kia-Ora squash for two days. He opened the bedroom door to investigate.

"Dada?"

"Chrissie? Are you all right, girl?"

"I'm fine. The excitement. This sadness, all this sadness."
She looked terrible. She was going to cry again.

"I'll make a cup of tea for you, my love."

"We'll both go down."

He took her by the arm and they descended the stairs

awkwardly. The all-night kettle was simmering on the back-burner of the range. He looked at her and began to worry. Her mother had said that she had been off-colour for the previous few weeks. Maybe it was the lieutenant. He wondered. Maybe things weren't working out after all.

"It's just a summer bug," Chrissie assured him.

"I hope you haven't picked up anything from Ellie."

"Only the marriage bug," Chrissie said.

"How's Barry?"

"He's the kindest person in the world," Chrissie said with intensity. "One thing you can be sure of, we understand each other. We talk about everything. I never met anyone who's so good at listening. He would never ask me to do anything I didn't want to do."

"Sure, I know he's a good lad."

"It's not easy being a doctor and an officer," Chrissie went on. "He might be transferred at any time. Companies are always moving around, and he's really attached to the motor squadron. It can be very lonely."

"How is he?"

"Fine, fine," Chrissie said. They sat down together and supped quietly. Outside the kitchen the morning declared itself with more vigour. Sparrows and house martins flitted and chatted across the yard. The Deputy looked at his daughter and was worried: she *did* look very pale. The strain of the last two days, Bobby's death and the heartbreak of her mother had taken their toll. He was pouring a second cup of tea for himself when he heard footsteps on the stairs. It was Adele coming to join them. She took a cup and saucer from the white press in the corner near the window. When she turned round they could see that her eyes were on fire. But no tears.

"Adele," said the Deputy, standing up to give her the only kitchen chair with a cushion.

❧

Bobby's funeral was the biggest spectacle that the town had seen in forty years. The coincidence of fair day and funeral created a crowd of over a thousand mourners. The spectacular unhappiness of the event, the death of a Deputy's first-born, made it immensely attractive to the poorer country people, small farmers from the mountains, river poachers and licensed fishermen, the casual labourers and their wives. They were also the natural power-base of the Party. They had seen the Deputy prosper since he moved into the district and married the coquettish daughter of a Free-State supporter twenty years before. They wondered if the death of his son was a watershed, a plateau from which his fortunes could only decline.

Bobby's coffin was draped in the dark blue flag of the rowing-club, and it was carried by the oarsmen he coached. Forty-eight priests from the seminaries of the diocese, garbed in funeral black, walked immediately behind the Glenville family. Every politician from the five neighbouring constituencies, one hundred political careers in all, marched behind the superior-looking men of God.

"I wanted to see his body," Adele cried weakly when they lowered the coffin into the velvet-lined grave. "I wanted to see all of my son."

The Deputy held her firmly. "You couldn't, love."

"I wanted to."

"Wasn't he lovely going out the door? Isn't it nice to remember him like that?" he pleaded. Bobby's face had been torn and made grotesque by the accident. It was Ned Kenny who persuaded them to keep Adele away from the body until the Deputy came home from Dublin. The Deputy then decided that Adele couldn't see her dead son. It was too horrific.

Young Gerald tugged at the sleeve of Adele's black dress. "Mama, I want to go to the toilet."

"Run over into the bushes," Emer said. They began to say the rosary.

"I want to do it at home. Too many people are looking," Gerald insisted.

"Go off into the bushes," Declan said. "Here, I'll take you." The two sons burrowed through the crowd in search of relief. When the rosary was over the family lined up by the graveside in traditional fashion. They prepared for the onslaught of handshakes.

"Oh, Mama!" Chrissie turned and wept on her mother's shoulder. Her young lieutenant in full uniform stretched out to hold her.

"We must accept God's will," Adele said.

"Mama!" Chrissie repeated. What her mother didn't know was that Chrissie was already pregnant with the twins whose energy would more than fill Adele's life until she died.

"Mrs Glenville, I'm very sorry," a dishevelled labourer said after the hundred or so politicians had passed on. "I often watched him on the river. He had a powerful stroke."

Adele recognised the man through her tears. He was a farm labourer called "The Warrior," who brought them a load of timber every autumn. "Thanks, Patey," she said, calling him by his real name.

Later they would pass "The Warrior" on his ass and cart, making his way home to the cottage in Chanley's wood. "Another donkey," the Deputy said. "I wonder where he got his hands on that old beast? If those donkeys could talk, they'd tell us a lot about ourselves."

ॠ

It was a week after Bobby's funeral, on 26 August, 1943, that Sir John Keane lost his seat in the Senate. He failed to attract even one vote on the Industrial and Commercial Panel, despite his brilliant Senate contributions on almost every aspect of business since the foundation of the state. His defeat marked a distinctive break in Irish politics: he had been the most articulate Unionist in the south. Throughout the war he was a staunch supporter of the Allied cause, a critic of political and moral censorship and, at times, the only voice of true opposition in the country. The ethos of neutrality and the native Catholic bourgeois interests had combined to exclude him.

The Deputy met Sir John outside Sargent's garage on the day after his Senate defeat. Sir John seemed unperturbed and philosophical. "The Senate doesn't matter that much anyway," the Deputy said.

"I feel that the country's brain has atrophied, you know.

I mean, you haven't been able to do much, have you?"

"Not much," admitted the Deputy. "But we've survived dangerous years."

"The greatest danger has passed. Even Sweden, which is dangerously close to Germany, has banned Germans on leave from using their railway network. It's a sign of the times."

"Dev is very legalistic. He has the mind of a lawyer."

"You mean the mind of a provincial schoolmaster," Sir John replied.

"Ah well," muttered the Deputy. A small crowd had gathered at the garage to watch the two Olympians at play. Sir John and the Deputy were rarely seen together. They belonged to different camps. The Deputy watched Ned Lonergan ambling along the footpath towards them; a poor peddler called Tom Poole and a county council employee called Mr Brackett were leaning against the rail at Sargent's window, listening with interest. "The Germans are still a powerful people," the Deputy said.

"Not now. Not since the Russians came in. They've pinned down fifty German divisions near Kharkov. Fifty divisions!" Sir John was full of war details. The provincial world of neutrality was not his. He had devoured reports of the Anglo-American conference in Quebec. All the signs suggested that the Allies had abandoned the idea of finishing the war by strategic bombing. President Roosevelt had given an inspiring speech to the Canadian parliament. There was talk of an army of ten million men to invade northern Europe. "The tide has turned," Sir John said. "It's such a blessed relief."

"There's still shortages here. They'll get worse as the Allies prepare for the invasion. There's going to be a government order to acquire metal."

"I see you have done a bit of gathering in yourself," Sir John teased the Deputy. The small crowd laughed. They loved to see a man caught while trying to pull a stroke.

"Business is tough," the Deputy explained. "I want to have enough materials to keep my men in jobs." He smiled.

"Well, men," Ned Lonergan came up to them and greeted them.

"Splendid day," said Sir John. "Is business slow?"

"I like to take a break. A man has to have some respite." Ned explained his desertion of his tailor-shop.

"I see."

"Christ, it's that Ryall, the traitor," Ned shouted, when he saw Mick L Ryall, the relentless reporter, approaching from the Barrack Street direction. Ryall was carrying a small Kodak box-camera.

"The perfect group," Mick said. "I bought the camera second-hand from Mr Hicks. He put a film in it. Willie Doyle said he'd print my shots."

"Go away, Mick," Ned Lonergan said.

"Would you prevent a man from earning his living?" Mick asked.

"You know nothing about cameras."

The Deputy rounded on him before he could humour the company. "You let us down badly during the election campaign. You reported on bullocks when you should have reported our speeches."

"Bobby had a lovely voice...a lovely voice," Mick replied.

"I've written a beautiful obituary."

"I'm very grateful," the Deputy said. The tone of his voice had softened at the mention of his son's name.

"Well, come along then, take your photograph," Sir John said impatiently. Mick's familiarity was offensive, especially since he was one year behind in his rent. The Deputy and Sir John posed reluctantly.

ॐ

Alice walked into the Glenville house. "Peace to all here," she said in an acquired country manner. "The Deputy and Sir John Keane are above at Sargent's garage being photographed by Mick Ryall."

Then Ellie came through the door. Her hair was tossed and the thinness of her face exaggerated the largeness of her eyes. "His shirts," she said. "I've taken off all the buttons." She was holding Bobby's shirts, destined for the Red Cross for use as bandage material. The buttons were saved; buttons were in short supply.

"You mustn't do too much, Ellie. Not while you're still on the mend."

"I know." She put the shirts down, but stooped over them, leaning on her elbows. "Oh, God, the shirts. They make me so sad."

Adele moved to her. "Strength, girl. God is good."

ॐ

That same weekend Justice McCabe, sitting in Waterford, refused to grant a licence for an area exemption to the publicans of Tramore. An open golf tournament was due to take place, but the judge decided that it wasn't a special occasion. "Quite a few young ladies were seen in a state of intoxication in Tramore during hours in respect of which exemption orders applied," he said. Few of the publicans appreciated his flowery language, but they understood what the words meant—loss of income. The judge's decision ended the Deputy's brief period of mourning. The phone hopped. Demands for action.

"Business is bad. Who does he think he is?"

"I gave you my number one. I've always supported your Party."

"You must bring this to the attention of the minister. What about the effect on the holiday trade?"

In all, the Deputy received twelve letters and eight phone-calls. He could do nothing. The old story. He would write a letter to the minister and a letter seeking clarification from the tourist board. He would get standard replies. He would send letters to Tramore quoting the replies from official sources. But the publicans' anger would subside.

❧

One evening, the Deputy, Captain Mulvey, Alice and Chrissie, went for a walk by the river. "Isn't it beautiful?" Alice said, looking downriver at the tall ridge of deciduous trees. They heard the sound of a mechanical saw. Someone was working in the woods near Killehala. It might have been "The Warrior."

The evening sky held their attention; a sky that had

changed from rain-shower black to August blue even while
they walked. The afternoon left vaporous streaks of red
and orange on the southern horizon. It was as if a coastal
anti-aircraft unit had fired a pattern of star-shells to mark
the neutral territory.

"Yes, it is beautiful now," the Deputy said. He looked
at Chrissie. "It reminds me of the first day I came into this
town. I met your mother on that road. She was wearing a
tight red dress. I'll never forget it. And I had a few hundred
pounds in my pocket. A small fortune then."

"It's still a small fortune," Captain Mulvey said. "I'd
love to be young again."

"Why?" Chrissie asked.

"Because the world will be a great place after the war.
Free trade everywhere. A paradise for the merchant marine."

"Do you believe that?" the Deputy asked.

"I know it." His cocker spaniel, Moll, came out of the
water carrying something in her mouth.

"What's that?" asked Chrissie, horrified. "Has she killed
a bird?"

"Not at all. It's only a brown paper bag." He called the
spaniel. She dropped the empty bag. It lay on the grass.

"Like the one that started the race," Chrissie said,
thinking of Bobby.

"Hell hath no fire like a publican burned," Captain
Mulvey said suddenly. He was interested in the plight of
the Tramore publicans. He thought the judge had been
rather hard. "I suppose they've been pestering you?" he
asked the Deputy.

"Pestering me? I'm demented from them," the Deputy replied.

"You should give up that old Dáil," Chrissie suggested. She stumbled on a tuft of grass but regained her footing quickly. Captain Mulvey moved to help her. He seemed very concerned about her. Did he know? He was very worldly-wise. His heart had been broken in Gibraltar. She wondered if others knew. Soon she would have to tell the whole family. She wasn't in the least bit afraid. She was absolutely sure of herself. The love in her family was like a rock.

"No, no, you mustn't give up the Dáil," Alice said with all the fervour of one who was leaving. "You need the Dáil more than ever now."

"I think the love has died between you and Dev," Chrissie said. She looked at her father's ravaged face. He was still a young man, her father, only forty-three, but sorrow had furrowed his brow.

"I feel I should have done more for that IRA lad. He was so young. I expected more from Dev."

The Deputy looked across the river. A boat went by. It was one of the workers at the Villiers-Stuart estate, drifting back to Villierstown on the ebb-tide. The man waved. The Deputy and Captain Mulvey waved in response.

"I've heard nothing more from the Republicans about it. I thought they might make trouble. It's early days yet," he went on.

"Not at all," said Captain Mulvey. "They can see that you've suffered enough."

The Deputy looked at his daughter. An acknowledgement of pain. "If I had come home more often I might have helped my own son," the Deputy said, helplessly. "I wonder. I wonder would Bobby still be alive today?"

✿✿✿✿